dominion of the divine

j. s. nathaniel

Published in

denver, colorado

Illustrated by

cheyenne sandoval

also by j. s. nathaniel

Juliet + Juliette = Love in Mafia Land

Stardust Angel

Everything Spontaneous in the Land of Doll Parts

Primitive Beauty: Author's Sketchbook

contents

For the ones I would cross lifetimes to love again, this one lives because of you.

when mortals
touched the clouds

If a single tongue can unify people, then no horizon will hold them, no gate would bar them, no roof holds them. So let us descend and confuse their speech. That ear and mouth pass like strangers. And the Lord scattered them like seeds on the wind. Babel's skeleton loomed, half-forged under a sky that watched in silence. The tower rose in defiance, and with it, humanity broke.

preface

Hunter struck the sidewalk and shattered. Bone, blood, breath, scattered like code across fresh cobblestone. For a suspended heartbeat, the city held, neon frozen mid-gasp, a car horn trapped in its own echo. Then the world lurched forward, indifferent, devouring him in its mechanical roar.

In that final exhale, a latch gave way. Death didn't strike, it leaned in, a shadow intimate as a lover's kiss. Life uncoiled its chains, sloughing mortality like skin. A pinhole of light pierced the veil, beckoning him into the glitch.

He lifted his gaze, spires clawing a summer sky, broken fingers reaching for the moon, trying to climb out from the dark. Voices leaked from cracked windows, lost in siren choruses. Worshippers bowing to new gods on nightly walks, faces glowing with screen light.

In the beam, truth shed its skin too. The aliens' gifts were mere phantoms wrapped in manufactured marvels. Their war for souls already etched in the stars. As the last spark fled his eyes, Hunter crossed the threshold, into the unknown, where they lurked. Freedom's war was a fatal murmur beating inside every heart.

57: the mimic's debt

The Grandview climbed from traffic haze like exhumed ribs—ancient stone sheathed in honeycomb glass. Roman arches framing a grimy sidewalk where commuters squinted through brass carousel doors into the urban swarm. Alabaster pillars gleamed within, pristine as veneer teeth under the lobby's chandeliers. Spilling alien blood across that marble would sour champagne and caviar tongues in a dozen boardroom mouths.

A man with a briefcase sliced the lobby's light, precise as a scalpel. Hunter's gaze locked, unblinking. Alien executions were a patriotic duty. Not for country, but for humanity. Eliminating aliens demanded neural plugins that blocked their mind-reading probes and blending into the shadows. One whiff of his intent, and the timeline would coil backward, erasing hard-won gains in the blink of a cosmic eye. He'd danced those loops before, paid in rivers of blood and ghosts. Stains etched deeper than bone, sins outlasting stars. Rules etched in every fracture. Sever the head to spare the corpse. It applied to mimics. And aliens in human costumes, too perfect to be real, not a hair out of place.

He tailed the unremarkable figure onto the street. Clean distance was his ally against the morning rush. Commute jaws snapped shut, the sidewalk a vein pulsing bodies. He shouldered through, clipped elbows, surged as the target slipped. "Hey, watch it, asshole!" a voice snapped, the crowd devoured it, indifferent as the haze.

At the corner of thirty-second, Hunter reacquired the mimic gnawing on sludge wrapped in parchment, a falafel, maybe, or some street-vendor slop, briefcase hunkered between scuffed loafers like a dormant bomb. No one clocked the impostor inches from their elbows, humanity's perennial blind spot, ordinary and worn, a chink in the armor of normalcy.

The world ticked on, deceptively steady. No nanite tempests shredding flesh from bone. No temporal fractures freezing strides mid-lunge into grotesque tableaux.

"Eat up, parasite, this is your last meal," Hunter breathed, slipping into alley shade, his veil of anonymity. He hummed Moon Lullaby under his breath. Ember's voice threaded through him, glass-bell pure. *I see the world, and the world sees me.*

His eyes stung. She'd been his anchor, his north star in the void's carnage, until the mimics ripped her away in that fog-choked wreck. That battered case cradled the key to her cage, a digital loop holding coordinates, memories, whatever twisted salvation the aliens hoarded. He'd pry it free or die in the unraveling.

In the periphery, Hunter missed the blonde woman shadowing him. The mimic in scuffed loafers veered into the alley's gloom, drawn perhaps by some program glitch. Hunter struck without mercy, leg sweep low and vicious, the case tumbling like a bruised satellite to asphalt. The thing shrieked as pavement grated its borrowed cheek. Synthetic skin splitting to reveal iridescent under flesh. Hunter pinned the throat, hauling it skyward by the lapels. "Debt calls due," he growled, voice gravel in the throat. "You hollowed my world, now pay in rot."

The human suit slithered like oily scales under his grip. He tightened, veins bulging. The mimic's tongue lashed the air, as if siphoning Hunter's pheromones, "I taste so much pain in you, juicy as burger and fries."

"Yeah, you like that, you sick fuck?" Hunter spat, "I hope you choked on your Happy Meal before her final gasp in the mist."

"Gasp?" It rasped, eyes flickering with false empathy. "We bestowed eternity on the child. You're stuck in echoes and human meat. You contaminated the weave."

Dagger drawn from his boot sheath, the blade a hesitant shimmer, transmuting glass to alloy under the dappled light. The meteorite hilt veined with captive lightning The alien jerked back, its skin glitching like a corrupted feed. "Trinkets," it rasped, laughter slithering through its static voice. "You don't need trinkets. You're one of us... unless you've already lost the gift."

"Grateful we're not in the Dall," Hunter murmured, the Dall a death sentence. "One wish there, and you're cinders in the void."

He thrust clean and surgical. The strange alloy burrowed through mimic meat, questing for the core. No ripple of variance. No timeline tear sucking reality inward. It bubbled wetly, "Without us, you're a specter in fixed loops, haunting your own irrelevance."

A chime pierced the din, two notes, high then low, like a dirge in binary. The briefcase stirred on the ground, latches parted with a sigh, light throbbing inward to fifty-seven seconds. Flesh glitched before him. Female-form warping to serpent coil, then dissolving to hairy-snow, a cone of glitter sifting to the pavement in mocking silence.

A voice needled his skull, sterile and digital, laced with synthetic pity: *REMAKING YOU, MR. PERSEFONI. SUPERIOR TO FRAIL FLESH, OPTIMIZED FOR THE WEAVE.*

He lunged for the hilt, it reciprocated, nanites swarming like silver ants, burrowing under skin, searing three interlocking chevrons into his palm like a brand from the stars. Heat snaked upward to his temple, a fever uncoiling. "It won't be long now," he murmured, tasting copper victory. The number plunged. Fifty-six seconds.

A blast erupted without warning. Vision blinding into supernova fury. Nanites flowering through bone like poisonous roots. Language unraveled in his throat. Towers warped in languid swells, the skyline bending like heated glass. The sun held steady overhead, ordinary, a lone plane slicing the blue. Normality's cruel anchor yanking the skew into sharper relief. Nausea nailed him to the alley wall, black blood crowned his collar in cold machine blur.

The glitter cone mocked from the ground, inert now, a fool's pyre. "Mine?" he slurred, fingers probing the cold drips at his scalp, slick as oil. Knees folded under the onslaught. Sparks fractured his sight into prismatic shards. Numerals pulsed faint against the haze. Fifty-five seconds. The latch whispered open once more. Chimes echoed, high, low. Breath ghosted his nape, chill as a lover's sigh in the grave. He smiled into the encroaching void, hand reaching for a phantom grasp, "Ember, I'm no longer a ghost in the weave."

The count dropped. In that final tick, Hunter glimpsed the weave's cruel lie. Not salvation in the case, but another fracture, pulling him deeper into the mimics' eternal debt. The alley swallowed him whole, humanity's blind spot closing like a noose.

The number fell.

53: echoes in the glitch

Light seared everything. No edges. No confines. An expanse of white that breathed like a living lung, inhaling the remnants of Hunter's fractured world. He blinked into awareness. Body knit whole again. The alley's blast a fading memory. Another failed attempt. Another scar tacked to a mind that refused to let go of every laugh, every whisper, as sharp as the day he heard them last.

The glitter cone of the mimic's dissolution piled neatly, the nanites branding his palm with interlocking chevrons, they lingered as ghosts, but the street's chaos had vanished. Blood no longer warmed his collar. The countdown's cruel tick had paused at fifty-three seconds.

He stood, boots silent on an invisible floor. The air still humming with sterile victory. At the chamber's core sat the briefcase, a matte, obsidian wound against the glow. Its latches sealed like a mimic's eyes. Hunter's hand twitched toward it, the fresh tattoo throbbing, a map to Ember, or another trap in the aliens' endless game. "Do you have a soul?" he rasped, his voice swallowed by the sterile abyss. "You animals! How could you cage my baby like this?"

The case didn't stir, but voices bloomed from the radiance. Alien harmonies overlapping, a chorus of silk-wrapped barbs: *WE UNVEILED HER TRUTHS. UNVEILED YOURS.* Their tones slithered, mocking the human frailty they mimicked so well: *DID YOU BEHOLD IT, MR. PERSEFONI? THE CODE STRIPPED BARE.*

Ember's scream ignited behind his eyelids, a fresh horror awaited him. The Volvo's crumple. Her small form limp in the fog-shrouded wreckage. Tara's final gasp clawed through. Her eyes wide with that desperate plea. *Save her. Please, my daughter.*

The memory hit like a timeline fracture, splintering his resolve. "All lies!" Hunter snarled, fists clenching until nails bled palms. "I'll stuff that human Happy Meal right down your fucking—"

A feminine chill threaded his veins, precise as code injection: *REALITY IS THE ACHE YOU CARRY. IT LINGERS SUFFICIENTLY, DELICIOUSLY. THIS IS THE NATURE OF THE WEAVE.* The light convulsed. The chamber unraveled like faulty pixels, dissolving into lush expanse under an azure vault that stretched endlessly.

He stood before a meadow now. Hills undulating soft as breath and crowned with wildflowers. The air pricked with tangerine zest and pepper's bite. Ember's laughter danced on the wind. Her silhouette darting through the blooms, pigtails whipping like comet tails. She spun, her grin sun-carved.

C'mon, Daddy! Mommy's waiting!

Hunter's heart lurched. He lunged, snaring her hand, fingers fragile as bird bones, warm pulse thrumming life. Heat cascaded through him, mending cracks in his grief. For a breath, the weight of war lifted. Timelines aligning in this stolen weave.

They ran, petals bursting underfoot like muffled firecrackers. Her giggles were armor against the void's roar. But her grip slacked and slipped free, blooming into the field. Petals bowed in mournful salute as silence collapsed all around, devouring her echo.

"Ember!"

The shout tore free, raw as the day she died. Light dimmed, the horizon crinkled like burning film. When clarity pierced the sky, Tara stood, adrift in currents, palms framing his face. It splintered everything inside him, betrayal's kiss before the crash, the aliens' 'gifts' that twisted love to ash. *Flee this illusion.* Tara's murmur brushed the back of his mind. Her eyes pools of fading gold.

"Come with me," he said, voice cracking. "I won't abandon you again."

Her luminescence flickered, edges fraying. *Lingering means erasure. Yours.* Ours.

A beam swept the gloom, a lighthouse tossed into the abyss. Each arc erasing her form. Hair to vapor. Skin to ember-glow. He clawed for her, she guttered out. LEAVE, NOW.

A strange darkness washed over him, poisoning him like nanites. Somewhere cloaked in the blackness, a drone that graduated into a haunting shriek, burrowing skull-deep, lightning yanking him through chronal rifts. Years collapsed in vertigo, back to nine, his father's den. Aldebaran Persefoni hunched over schematics, ghost-weaver of timelines, deliberate as betrayal. Pain always vectored here, a gravitational scar.

The first fist landed, methodical, lesson one: love and hate, indistinguishable in the dark. A second cracked ribs, blood coppered the air. Aldebaran's eyes, cold as meteorite, bored in. *Weakness invites the fracture, boy. Mend or shatter.*

Bone cracking against bone echoed. *Shatter it is.*

Even now, those gore-smeared hands clawed across time, hauling Hunter into the bruise's eternal loop. Strikes blurred, past echo or present haunt? Fire lashed jaw and gut, surrender whispered, a siren's glitch in the neural storm. The aliens' voices overlapped his father's growl, "We remake the flawed."

But Tara's plea pierced the maelstrom. *They feed on your weakness. Fight their weave.*

One ragged inhale, defiance's spark, and the plummet resumed. Glass rained phantom shards, the city bleached to white once more.

In the distance, where life stacks neatly, the sound of a whistle mingling with the hush. His father's tuneless dirge, an invader's signal, his own fractured sigh, shattered to nullity. Death didn't claim him, it chaperoned, ushering through the glitch's maw. Silence bloomed, absolute. Then a voice sliced the glare, clinical as an autopsy saw: *AWAKEN, MR. PERSEFONI. YOUR DESCENT CONCLUDES. THIS STOP IS WHERE THE REAL DESCENT BEGINS.*

The chamber reformed, briefcase pulsing faint. Fifty-four seconds now. The count resuming its programmed march in reverse. Hunter's eyes fluttered like scattered birds. Nanites hummed dormant in his veins, chevrons itching like fresh brands. The aliens' war wasn't for skies or souls, but the marrow of memory itself, rewriting fractures into obedience. He rose, hand closing on the case's icy handle. Ember's laugh ghosted one last time. Not salvation, but spur. In the white's indifferent breath, he stepped forward, whole yet hollow, into the loop's next coil. Freedom? A myth in mimic skin. But resistance burned eternal, since the rise.

54: mr. fall

He hit the floor screaming. Glass rained with him, shards hissing through white, static air. Though, the impact never came. Sound warped. Gravity deserted the world. The city dissolved into an alien light. Somewhere, a whistle followed him down. His father's, the alien's, his own, until it fractured into nothing. Then stillness. Death sat beside him again, quiet and patient.

"Time to wake up, Mr. Persefoni. This is your stop."

He gasped awake to pain. The second blow cracked his jaw. Bone sang low and rich, ligaments returning home. No time was spared as another followed. His eyes opened to a blur. Colors bleeding into each other. Exhaust trailing the edges of everything and nothing. A figure loomed above him. Its voice was metallic, practiced and unhurried.

"There he is. You gave us quite a scare. Torture's on the menu today, I'm afraid. Drastic measures, as you say."

Hunter strained to focus, his lashes fluttering like startled birds. The light behind the creature flared like a dying star. "I'm up," he groaned.

"Good of you to join us. A smack here, a smash there, it clears the garbage upstairs." Laughter electrocuted him like static.

He tested his arms, and they were shackled. Or maybe only his mind was. Cuffs bit into his wrists, etched with alien script. Naked and exposed, the dagger no longer in reach, shame began to burn inside him, hotter than fear.

"Trinkets," the alien said, admiring the dagger as it pulsed with liquid light. "Always so resourceful. But you of all people know, we can't risk losing another Time Recorder."

Hunter bared his teeth, black blood threading down his chin, "Say we again. I dare you."

Another voice, female, perfect, rehearsed, cut in. "We admire your work, Mr. Persefoni. Truly. But your appetite for death is distorting the weave. What will become of it."

Three identical blondes emerged from the glare. High cheekbones. Mirror eyes. Beauty engineered to disguise the rot underneath.

Hunter laughed, ragged. "Triplets, cute. I was worried this might get boring."

One smiled. "Contrary to what you think, we don't celebrate human executions. Too many variables. The weave must maintain a predicable algorithm. But you have something we need."

"What, my sparkling personality."

"You're stuck in a time loop, Mr. Persefoni. The future yet to come." Her tone iced. "Help us recalibrate the weave and we'll return your wife and child."

Tara's name detonated in his chest, "Lies," he whispered.

"Try us, Mr. Persefoni."

Pain hit him lightning fast. His body seized. Teeth chattered. "You see?" she slithered. "Obedience is freedom."

Hunter slumped forward, he could barely think. Tara's voice whispered inside him, defiant. *They prey on your heart. Strike now, before it's too late.*

Hunter spat blood and grinned, "Bring them back. That's the deal."

The aliens circled him like hunters who'd already decided where to place the knife. "Wise," the center one said. "This is not a timeline to be stuck in."

The cuffs snapped open. Metal peeled away like bark from wet wood, leaving welts glowing beneath his skin. A faint shimmer moved under the surface, scales, barely there.

He looked down. Scales shimmered faintly across his wrists. "Look what you did, you parasites."

Her smile didn't reach her eyes. "We only reminded you of what you are."

Symbols flared across the tablet they carried, scripts glowing like molted glass. "If you break the connection, we all die. If we die, they die."

"Then, let's dance," he said.

Black static filled the air. The scent of thunderstorms and citrus bled into his nose. Machines screamed until the sound turned silent. The tablet flared, feeding on his memories.

Sea salt. Funerals. Ember's laughter. Tara's whisper. *It's a trick.*

An alien smiled. "She whispered your name seven times in her final moments. Across four different timelines. Do you know why?"

Rage broke loose inside him, like a storm ripping the sky in two. He pulled against the device, knowing he might not get another chance. Shockwaves rippled through the room. Plasma lifted the aliens, slammed them into walls, pinned them like dolls.

The key to captivity lied in alien hands, yet he pulled toward annihilation anyway. "Give me strength!"

The tablet shrieked. Light poured through the seams of reality. A voice thundered inside his skull. *Come find me. I am the door.*

He smiled through inky blood, excretion from machines. "I see you."

Tara's silhouette rose from the glare. *Follow my voice.*

"My life for yours," he whispered, and wrenched free.

Energy exploded. The aliens screamed. Cosmic fire devoured them, leaving only glitter where bodies had been. Hunter collapsed, laughing and weeping all at once.

"You bleed," he rasped. "Only difference, your ashes sparkle."

Dust rained from the ceiling. Cracks split the walls. He grabbed the tablet and ran.

Outside, dawn cleansed the city anew. He stumbled through the streets, bare, bloodied, wrapped in wire and plastic. A billionaire reduced to penniless form. He reached his tower before sunrise. Through the lobby. Up the stairs. Into the penthouse. The maintenance door glowed with a slit of light. He set the tablet on the threshold and felt lighter, almost free.

Upstairs, the shower scalded him. Black residue spiraled down the drain like confession. He whistled a tune he swore he'd never whistle again—his father's. When he looked in the mirror, his reflection laughed. Not his face. Hers. The blonde alien.

"You're dead," he whispered. "I watched you die."

She smiled from the glass. "There's no escaping this, Mr. Persefoni. There never was."

Scales shimmer across his skin. He screamed and ran for the window. Glass shattered around him as he plunged from the eighteenth floor. Above, the alien strolled to the window, listening for the wet thud. When it came, faint, final, she grinned.

"What a waste, Mr. Persefoni. Your best performance yet."

She whistled his tune as her body flickered into starlight and vanished.

49: fog's reckoning

The night fractured first. Wind punched his chest as the window shattered outward. Glass followed him down, shards whispering through the cold air.

Hunter embraced the fall. He had done this before. In another life. In another loop. The city tilted, lights folding into white blur. He thought of Ember's hair glowing against a kitchen window, Tara's laugh echoing in the dark.

The ground rose to meet him. But the impact never came. Sound warped. Gravity slipped. The city dissolved into light. Somewhere, a whistle followed him down, until it broke into static.

Then, stillness. Death beside him again.

"Tragic, yes," the voice hissed through the ether, a serpent's tongue slithering inside his skull. "Such accidents keep the world tidy. Statistics, Mr. Persefoni. Numbers you'd appreciate, if you understood the weave."

Darkness peeled away like ancient wallpaper, unveiling a stretch of highway. Ordinary at first glance, cracked concrete, faded yellow lines snaking into the haze. Heat vapors dancing. But Hunter's stare lingered, and a new reality bled in. The scene stuttered, rewound on invisible reels, then lurched forward with the devil's revenge.

A black SUV erupted from the shimmer. No headlights piercing the gloom. Windshield a void of polished coal. It rammed the Volvo's bumper with surgical nudge, recoiled, then prowled again, a panther toying with wounded prey. "Look closer," the voice coaxed, silk over rot. "Let's etch the details eternal."

The Volvo devoured miles under Tara's white-knuckled grip. His family cocooned in vinyl and false safety. Mist crept first as a distant veil, until it found them. Then the sky closed like a coffin lid, dimming the world into gray. Wind battered the station wagon sideways, forcing it into the right lane. Ember heard air slip through the window seal, soft whistles, like ocean waves beckoning from the deep.

"Can we, Mommy? Can we go to the beach?" Ember sang, oblivious to the gathering chaos knocking at the window.

"The beach?" Tara echoed.

Fog cascaded over asphalt like milk over ash. Headlights shimmered within, devouring the road's edge. Tara ignited every lamp, defying Hunter's warning. *Low beams in mist, always.* He'd been right in saner hours, but tonight, sanity vanished into the mist.

In the rearview, Ember's tablet bathed her cheeks in cool glow, then Tara's pulse spiked, a black SUV tailing too close for coincidence. No lights. Windshield blackened to nothing. Cold questions struck. Why no headlights? Why was the windshield blacked out?

Tara had seen people who weren't quite people following them around the airport, but she believed it was her mind playing tricks on her. She hadn't slept well in days.

The SUV blared, brights flaring. Tara muttered, "What do you want, asshole?"

"What's an asshole?" Ember asked, head tilting, tablet forgotten.

The word lodged bitter. The beast clung to their bumper, weaving taunts, flashing brights relentless. Tara veered right, praying it would pass. Instead, it lunged shoulder-side, gravel erupting like gunfire against steel. The wagon shuddered, the black shape dissolved into gray. "What a jerk," Tara said, voice small against the roar.

The silenced pooled thick. "Mommy, those ladies look really mad," Ember murmured, gaze drifting.

Tara's brow furrowed. "The driver's a woman?"

"Yeah, their eyes are shiny."

"Shiny?"

"They glow."

Tara whipped to the mirror. For a heartbeat, she saw them too. Two pale beams seeping through the SUV's tinted windows, then fog claimed them. Their world reduced to blur, her heart thudded. Creepy ladies with luminous stares, now trapped in their wake. *Way to go*, she thought.

Then Hunter's voice intruded—the argument, the kiss, the betrayal he'd called an accident. That had hurt worse than the act itself. Not knowing meant he could do it again.

The SUV resurfaced, lights jittering lanes like hunting hounds. Tara's knuckles bleached. "What do you want?" she breathed to ghosts.

"They're laughing," Ember said, unblinking. "Laughing?" The tablet's glow mirroring the malice.

The SUV's horn shattered the hush. Tara wrenched the wheel as the beast skimmed, shrapnel pelted. "Don't look, honey," she said.

The mist turned to a living wall. Headlights warped inside it, strange colors flickering like a prism. The Volvo inched forward, tires gnashing debris. In the mirror, three sets of eyes gleamed through tinted glass. Eyes too bright to be human.

Ahead, carnage bloomed. Vehicles mangled, beams bent, smoke tendrils coiling. Tara seized Ember's hand. "Down, baby. Low as you go."

The SUV circled, lights pulsing mockery.

"Mommy, are we playing a game?"

"No, baby. No games."

The dash screamed. Warning lights flared, a digital voice whistle through the car speaker, *Brake system failure. Steering offline. Goodbye.* The Volvo spun. Glass exploded. The world turned over itself. Ember's tablet tumbled like a strobe. Her scream cutting through the chaos. Impact. The station wagon stopped upside down. Tara hung in her harness, choking on smoke and melted plastic. She clawed at the buckle. Nothing.

"Ember!"

"My arm, Mommy."

"Press the button, baby, Mommy's stuck."

"I'm scared."

"I know you can do it, be brave!"

A faint click echoed inside the interior. Ember's body landed with the sound of bone-crack. Her wail pierced the looming danger outside. Tara wrenched the buckle that refused to click free. "Fuck."

Outside, hell roared. A horrifying symphony of screeching tires, crumpling metal, and voices swallowed by the mist. The metal card, she thought, the idea slicing through the screams.

Her hand plunged into her pocket. The restraint snagging movement. She yanked harder, her shoulder popping with a wet, sickening crack. Fire bloomed in her joint, but she pressed on, fingers grazing the cool edge, slipping, then hooking firm.

The knife, disguised as a credit card, flicked open with a whisper of steel. She sawed at the belt, the blade biting into her palm, shredding skin to small ribbons. Blood dribbling in warm splatters across the roof. One final, desperate tug, and the strap reeled high-speed.

She plummeted to the ceiling, the knife plunging into her ribs. Adrenaline dulled the agony to a distant throb. Hands and knees coated in shards, she crawled to Ember. Her daughter dangled there, limp as a broken toy. One arm twisted at an unnatural angle, swollen and purple.

"No." The word tore from Tara's throat as she hacked through Ember's belt, fibers fraying under the blood-slick blade. She hauled her daughter free, dragging her through the shattered hatch into the swirling fog.

The highway stretched as a graveyard of twisted hulks. Cars flipped like discarded toys. Flames guttering through the mist, screams fracturing the gray.

"Duck," a voice urged from deep within, primal and sure.

Tara jerked Ember down just as a green truck somersaulted overhead, its frame spinning in lazy arcs before smashing into the guardrail with a thunderous bang.

"That's it," Tara panted, her breath ragged. "We'll be safe over there."

Ember's eyes swam in blood, a raw pink welt swelling across her forehead. "I don't feel good, Mommy."

Tara's throat tightened, the lump appeared weblike. "Climb on my back. I'll carry you."

Ember latched on, her small arms feeble around Tara's neck. But the knife in Tara's chest twisted with the motion, heat flaring white-hot. "Slide off!" she gasped.

The blade had burrowed deeper than she'd realized, a lethal blow. Gritting her teeth, she seized the handle and wrenched it free. Agony exploded through her torso, a supernova of nerves igniting. She screamed, crumpling to the ground.

"Mommy!"

Tara hauled herself up, limbs quaking like branches taxed under wet snow. "I'm okay. Get on. We don't have much time."

"I'm scared."

"Listen to me." Tara cupped Ember's face, her voice an anchor amid purgatory. "We're going to make it. We'll see Daddy again."

Ember clung tighter, her weight fragile as a feather lost to wind. Tara lurched forward, lungs searing, the world a shrieking blur of death around them.

They staggered past a mangled truck. A man dangled upside down within, neck kinked at a fatal angle, mouth agape in silent accusation.

"Mommy, is he going to die?"

"Yes."

"Can we help him?"

"We can't."

Tara scaled the guardrail, every step a grind of will, and collapsed into the damp grass, cradling Ember close. Blood oozed warm between her fingers. She refused to glance at the wound.

"We made it," she murmured, the words a fragile lie.

But Ember's gaze had turned inward, distant as fading stars, her eyelids drooping heavy.

"Ember." Tara's plea cracked. "Don't go to sleep."

"Okay," Ember whispered, her voice a small echo.

Tara rocked her gently, humming the lullaby through choking sobs, the melody fracturing like wind rattling glass. The fog parted in reluctant wisps, unveiling the sprawl of wreckage and the distant wail of sirens. Salvation, maybe threading the dark.

"Do you hear that?" Tara breathed, hope flickering. "They're coming."

Ember's lashes fluttered once, a final butterfly wing, then stilled forever.

Tara's breath snagged, a sob trapped in her chest. She pressed her forehead to her daughter's cooling one and whispered, "I love you."

The sirens swelled, nearer now. For a heartbeat, that flicker of hope burned bright, until the black SUV erupted from the fog, scaling the wrecked truck like an Evil Knievel leap.

It hurtled skyward, headlights searing like twin suns. Tara froze, time splintering. She held Ember in her arms and hummed the lullaby. Tears carving hot trails down her cheeks. The SUV plummeted. Darkness claimed them both.

before death

Hunter emptied his pockets into the luggage. His left palm throbbed. He flexed his fingers, watching the interlocking chevrons shimmer beneath his skin. The nanite tattoo had been dormant for weeks. Now it pulsed faintly. Each beat synchronized with the weave. Maybe alerting him to another rogue time loop.

Fifty-three seconds until alignment.

The rhinestone clip Ember made glittered under the terminal lights. A child's craft glued over old power. Once, gold Cartier meant control. Now, her handmade carnival trinket sat where power used to live.

The attendant at the concierge station smiled. Words filtered through static. Tagged. Capsuled. *Enjoy your flight.* Her face slid from memory before Hunter even turned away. He tipped via neural ping, then pushed on through the terminal.

The terminal thrummed with quiet machinery, holographic images overhead, and foot traffic echoing against the terrazzo floor. A board flickered overhead to fifty-two. Hunter blinked. The number was gone, replaced by departure times. A trick of the eye, maybe. Or maybe not.

He almost bypassed the coffee exchange, but the air was thick with synthetic aromas. Coffee had transcended cheap adrenaline rushes and boardroom vigils that blurred into morning. Now, those engineered beans encoded decades, verging on centuries, distilled into a single costly, bitter sip. He ordered, neural pinged, held the cup like it might anchor him to gravity and claimed a seat facing the gate.

That's when the air bent.

Two men in black stood across the terminal. They didn't approach. They didn't have to. Darkness clung to their edges like motor oil, swallowing the ambient light. Their eyes found him with surgical precision. Not a stare. A procedure.

Obsidian shoes. Matte black. The same texture as the briefcase in the white chamber. The memory bit down hard. Ember's laugh echoing against sterile walls. The lullaby before the world split open. His palm seared. The chevrons flared to fifty-two. Not the usual speedy decent that had tormented him every day. It paused at fifty-two seconds, as though the alignment had abandoned the weave.

Hunter forced a sip. Too hot. Burned tongue. Strangely, the liquid wasn't tepid. *Swallow the pain. Stay small. Stay ordinary. Don't breathe too loud.*

The men raised their arms in unison, too accurate, too slow. A gesture without language.

"Yeah, I see you staring," he muttered.

He tried to look away, but the terminal looked staged, bright lights too bright, faces too smooth, like the world had rehearsed this scene without him.

The PA crackled overhead. A boarding announcement stuttered mid-sentence and restarted.

Alignment resumed at fifty-one seconds.

He bought another coffee, or maybe it was the same one. The barista leaned in, breath sweet like synthetic vanilla. "Do your friends want one too?"

"They're not with me."

"Those two? They want to be seen." Her voice bent at the edges. Her face fractured for a heartbeat, silky layers folding over each other.

Hunter turned, and they had vanished. Absence was louder than presence. His muscles braced for an impact that hadn't arrived yet. He scanned the crowd. Too ordinary. Too arranged. *Not real. Real enough.*

He cut through the terminal toward the gate. Two attendants unwound barrier straps, their movements deliberate, rehearsed. The taller one met his gaze with a perfect airline smile. Her turquoise lapel gleamed like living metal.

His palm flared. Her teeth stretched veneer white, her eyes reflecting a light that didn't exist, fifty. Blink. Human again. Or close enough.

The first-class cabin unfolded like a cathedral of light, glowing pods, soft pink and orange pulses, the hum of hidden machines. But Hunter didn't feel luxury. He felt lungs closing around him.

Julie's voice swam through syrup. Something about coffee. A gold wire cradle. His hands looked foreign wrapped around it. Through the oval window, mist moved across the runway snakelike. His reflection hung in the glass, slightly delayed. A half-second too slow. For a heartbeat, his reflection smirked while his real face stayed blank. *Not me. Me enough.*

Behind the reflection, two shadows stood in the aisle. He spun around to see nothing. But on the armrest, a card. Matte black. Obsidian. Fine black dust ringed its edges like the residue of something burned away. His pulse jumped. The chevrons writhed under his skin, eager. An Ouroboros. Three words beneath, unfamiliar yet understood in his marrow: *WE ARE INEVITABLE, MR. PERSEFONI.*

Forty-nine seconds.

The card dissolved into golden dust, coiling into interlocking chevrons above his palm. The weave. A child's voice, Ember's, whispered from somewhere behind the soundproofed cabin. *Don't let them in.*

But they already had.

The plane's boarding chime hiccupped, one tone eaten by static. Overhead, the cabin lights flickered once, like a held breath. Hunter pressed his palm against his chest. His heartbeat no longer belonged to him. It pulsed in time with the numbers. The world wasn't blinking anymore. It was waiting. *Not here.*

ALREADY INSIDE.

Breathe.

DON'T BREATHE.

He looked out the window again. The mist folded around the plane like a fist. His reflection tilted its head before he did. Its smile was not his. Obsidian dust glittered faintly on his palm. The countdown thrummed beneath the skin, beneath the floor, beneath the sky itself, Forty-nine seconds until alignment.

The weave closed its eyes. And Hunter's world forgot how to blink.

one

"I care about you, Evelyne," Hunter said, his voice cracking like glass underfoot. "Everybody wants this technology. They'll kill anyone who gets in the way."

Her face spoke volumes before words could form. Silence hung between them, thick as the San Francisco mist the plane would part from. A soft tremor moved through his palm. The chevrons. One faint beat, waiting.

The plane shuddered to a halt at LaGuardia, 3:39 p.m. Eastern Time. Julie, the attendant, stood at the exit with the pilot, their faces carved in grim marble. The pilot nudged her forward. "Um, Mr. Persefoni—"

Evelyne slid between them with easy grace. "He's busy," she said, her voice a blade sheathed in fine silk. "I've briefed him."

Julie shifted, unsettled, her eyes darting like trapped birds. The pilot retreated a step, as if afraid of an invisible contagion. "Sir, your—"

"Let's keep this a good flight." Evelyne's voice cut the air clean.

Relief softened the pilot's shoulders. "Of course. Your family is in our prayers."

Hunter didn't answer. He just nodded, trying to pretend those words meant nothing. But in our prayers? That wasn't protocol. It was the language of mourning dressed up as kindness. The words lodged in his chest, a dull blade twisting, sympathy laced with warning.

He trailed Evelyne through the jetway, her stride a magnet he resisted. Those chevrons pulsed warmer now, dangerous as the kiss they'd shared weeks ago. The one he'd confessed to Tara. The memory scorched. Her lips on his, electric, forbidden, then Tara's eyes, shattering like computer code.

The terminal opened around him in a gray static motion. People moved in slow, luminous waves. Blurs of coats and voices, a human tide eroding the edges of his world. Evelyne tried to veer off toward the office, but Hunter stopped her, "What about my luggage?"

"You should come with me."

Her green eyes caught the fluorescent glare, pulling him like gravity's cruel hook. He teetered on the brink, orbit destabilizing. He wanted her, still, after everything. But distance was his only armor. "I can't," he murmured, the words fragile as ash.

Her gaze pinned him, too long, too deep. Then she vanished, swallowed by the crowd.

Hunter snatched his suitcase, fumbling for his phone. Hands shook, the screen stayed dark. "Damn it." He hissed the curse low.

Wheels clacked over metal seams. Clack. Clack. Clack. The sound burrowed into his pulse, ascending from his soles. No longer wheels. A countdown. A fuse hissing toward detonation.

He scanned the terminal for Tara and Ember. Instead he saw Barbara and Mayer standing in the distance. A flicker at the far end of the terminal. Faces carved from grief. The luggage slipped from his hand. His mind gripped it still. He walked toward them without meaning to. Their faces sharpened the closer he got. Barbara wearing death like a mask she'd never take off. Mayer hollowed and pale. They didn't approach. He already knew. Without words. Tara and Ember were already gone.

He turned away. Mayer's hand caught Barbara, holding her back. No one crossed the distance. Not yet. The terminal lights flickered. Just once. Behind him, a digital board glitched forty-nine. Then snapped back to flight departure times.

Hunter's chest constricted. Electricity surged down his arm, chevrons igniting. Fingers buzzed, reality fraying at the seams. He quickened, but the pulse stalked. Clack. Clack. Clack. Energy clawed upward, into ribs, locking knees. Vision haloed, faces stretched into elongated phantoms under the buzz. In the throng, flickers, two figures in black. Shadows masquerading as men. Or voids given form.

A tremor seized his jaw, dragging his lip down. He strained to move. Couldn't.

The overhead speaker crackled, "...Gate—static—forty-eight..."

The air thinned to helium fragility. Gravity betrayed him. Hunter collapsed. The floor rushed up, embracing with brutal poise. The world whirled, a deranged carousel of lights and screams. Bystanders smeared into streaks. His hand clawed skyward, a reflexive plea, "Forgive me."

His heart squeezed. The chevron whispered in his palm. Once. Twice. Low. Patient. Forty-eight. Vision tunneled to a spark. Heartbeat. Number. Edges of the world drew inward, squeezing light to embers. Somewhere beneath everything, the countdown kept ticking. Not toward something. Toward him.

The spark went out. And the blackness collected him.

whisper between seconds

Fifty seconds. The whisper swam alongside the pulse. Not sound, but a tremor.

The black sedan waited under the garage lights, haloed by a sheen of gentle rain. Two guards bent over, examining Hunter's limp body, unsure whether to call an ambulance or a priest.

"That's Mr. Persefoni," Garry said. "Mr. McDermott's guest."

The guard's eyes widened, "Get an ambulance down here right now."

"No, don't," Garry snapped. "This happens sometimes. The guy lost his wife and kid."

The guard hesitated, fear and liability colliding, then finally growled, "If this comes back to me."

"It won't," Garry said. "I swear."

They loaded Hunter into the back seat. The luxury sedan pulled out like it was trying to outrun a bank heist.

Hunter came back to himself when the brakes screamed, tires skidding against wet pavement. The g-force pitched him against the floorboards. Garry cursed, slammed the horn.

A college student in a plastic lei and Mardi Gras beads spun drunkenly in the headlights, middle finger raised like a war flag.

Hunter stared at her through the window as the whisper crept up his wrist again. Forty-nine.

Not a number on a screen. A presence.

"Are we close?"

"Not much farther," Garry said. "We had to reroute."

The city celebrated around them, reflections in puddles stretching thin as thread, lights smearing into an abstract painting. Every passing shadow felt a beat off, like time stuttered whenever Hunter blinked. Alien static never leaving his side.

He saw Barbara and Mayer's faces in the fog of memory, pale echoes from the funeral they never attended. Their absence was a wound. And the wound had a shape, a black SUV.

The pileup was supposed to be impossible. In an automated world, cars didn't just *crash*. But someone had shoved a light-colored Volvo off the highway that night. No plates. No trace.

Just tire tracks, thick and brutal, biting into the mud.

The official line was an accident. But accidents didn't move with military precision.

They didn't erase thirty minutes of highway surveillance. They didn't leave paint chips belonging to a vehicle no one could find.

Hunter had thrown millions at the void. Lawyers. Investigators. Ghosts of men who once belonged to three-letter agencies. Every time they got close, they vanished. One analyst whispered a name before disappearing, Ouroboros. Forty-eight seconds. Another branch Hunter had never heard of, buried under layers of state secrets and clearances. Connected to The Dall. Connected to McDermott's Nano Company. An alien door beneath the floorboards. And silence behind it.

Hunter met his own eyes in the rearview mirror. His reflection lagged behind. He flinched.

"How much farther?" he said, the back of his palm wiping sweat from his forehead as if a fever had set in.

"We're almost there," Garry answered. He hesitated for a moment. "I lost my brother, his entire family a few months back. Gas leak at a resort. Killed them all. It only happened in that room."

Hunter clenched his jaw. The whisper rippled through the car like a heartbeat: Forty-seven seconds. The next thing he knew, he was in the helicopter. The rotors carved the night into ribbons. The pilot's voice cracked through the headset, "Mr. Persefoni. Southampton in thirty-three minutes. Sixty degrees. Unbelievable for this time of year."

He studied her profile, young at a glance, silvered at the edges. The air was thin and moldy. His heart matched the propeller's rhythm. Whirr forty-six. Whirr forty-five. Sleep threatened him again. But every time he slipped into darkness, they were waiting. Tara. Ember. Not ghosts. Not quite alive either. Stuck on pause in an alien world, caught between seconds.

The SUV investigation had led nowhere. Everyone used those black vehicles. That was the genius. They were perfect for the crime that didn't exist. "They're invisible," the investigator had said. "Too common to trace."

Those tracks, the ones carved in mud, still haunted his dreams. Hunter had promised himself he'd find the killer. He bribed. Blackmailed. Built a shadow network of analysts and ex-spooks. One by one, they disappeared. Only the analyst who whispered one word, the only word, had lasted long enough to leave a scar.

Another world had emerged from the fog. One without laws. One accountable to no one. A world that answered not to God, but to itself.

The helicopter tilted slightly, below him, Manhattan glittered like a machine pretending to be a city. Hunter pressed his forehead to the cold glass. His reflection hovered there like a man standing on the other side of time. The countdown burned through his veins, not louder, just closer. Forty-four.

Tara and Ember lived inside the space between ticks. The weight of their absence pressed against his ribcage like a second heart.

He remembered standing at the threshold of their house and walking away. The scent of their things was too dangerous to face. Memory was a minefield. One step too deep, and he'd never crawl out. He never went back.

The blades hammered overhead. Hunter stared into the night. Garry's voice was long gone now. Only the drone remained. Only the whisper: Forty-three seconds.

The number didn't belong to any watch. It was older than clocks. It wasn't ticking down time. It was measuring him.

He closed his eyes, not to rest, but to fall. And somewhere between seconds, the whisper smiled.

part one
graves

Hunter watched two caskets descend while the priest intoned Psalm 23 —"though I walk through the valley."

The watch on his wrist had stopped at **3:33**. It had stopped for weeks now. Months, perhaps. But something else was counting down. Six minutes burned behind his eyelids. *Six minutes until alignment.*

Earlier that morning, bulldozers had demolished three houses on Sea Cliff Avenue. They had sat in a row along the cliff, but the middle one had been their home. It perched highest, offering a clear view of the Golden Gate Bridge. Nothing inside would be spared. He leveled them all the same.

Their voicemails were the only luxury from the past, a mausoleum of souls. He kept the cell service active as proof that love and nightmares were real. On bad nights, Hunter called until blackout tucked him away.

The phone grew warm in his pocket now, nearly hot.

The demolition of his childhood home had been inevitable, like the cliff houses themselves. Months earlier, luck, as Hunter called it, had provided the means. A business deal had deposited a million dollars in his account. The negotiations took place in an abandoned warehouse three miles from the old address, and afterward he found himself driving past the block, the place that had given him everything and nothing.

He left the car and crossed the lawn. His shoes left no prints in the grass. Painful memories surfaced like bodies rising from the deep. For years, he had feared what lived beyond that door. The house stood in filthy glory. Windows dark, paint peeling. Some places left stains. Those blemishes clung to darkness the way people did.

"You still know how to torment, even after all this time," Hunter murmured.

He returned it to the earth, for his mother, who had died in the fire, for the neighborhood, for himself. He turned the lot into a community garden. If he could grow something meaningful and pure, he might erase the bad.

The numbers shifted, two hours, twenty-seven minutes. The countdown pulsed through his temples like a second heartbeat.

The fog didn't roll in from the Pacific. It climbed from the graves, from the demolished foundations, from places fog had no business being. The air tasted coppery.

The whisper had started at dawn. Or had it been sunset?

Chevrons pulsed through his veins, surfacing on his skin—alien, insistent. They throbbed with the rhythm of the countdown, marking time against his flesh.

The numbers flickered in the fog itself now, six minutes painted in the mist. His gums bled when he touched them. Salt and iron flooded his mouth. The coordinates screamed through his bloodstream, a weave pulling him toward something he couldn't see but knew was coming.

He sketched a garden on a paper napkin. Expansive zones suitable for alliums. Tara loved those flowers. They attracted butterflies. Lupines would bring Mission blues to the cliffside, enough to create an island visible from above.

When he looked down at the napkin, a detailed sketch appeared in his hand. He didn't remember drawing it.

The church bells rang at 5:47 p.m., thirteen minutes until alignment. The temperature dropped fifteen degrees in thirty seconds.

He remembered the day at the Botanical Garden in Golden Gate Park. Afterward, Ember had become obsessed. She sculpted butterflies, small ones, large ones, jeweled ones. Paper wings covered every surface until the entire house became wings.

Now he would finish her masterpiece, an island large enough to be seen from heaven.

The temporal displacement pulled at his bones, threatening to unravel him molecule by molecule. Blood dripped from his nose. He wiped it away and found his fingertips stained black, not red, the mark of crossing between worlds.

In the reflection of his car window, someone stood behind him. When he turned, no one was there.

Hunter intended to cross over, even if it meant desecrating every world between here and there. No alien or ghost could stop him. He needed to send an urgent message, and the only address on file was heaven. If Ember saw blue butterflies from up there, she'd know they were a gift from him.

Sending love to earthly beings required a message in a bottle. Sending a message to heaven required wings.

Six minutes and one second. The alignment was recalibrating. The numbers crawled across those gold-plated coffins like alien fingers.

The sky forgot how to be blue.

The portal opened.

Or maybe it had always been open, and he was only now learning to see it.

part two
the veil

He approached the manor after the helicopter touched down. Wild vines had swallowed the building, yet it emanated a strange glow, as though the damned thing bore an alien soul. His watch read 3:39. The second hand twitched backward.

A whisper crawled from the wet night: six minutes. Stronger now. His eyes twitched, downloading invisible code.

In the distance, the ocean collapsed. Hunter squeezed his eyes shut and drifted away. Fishy water rushed back. Wet sand clumped between her toes. Every salty breath belonged to her. When he channeled her ghost, she was there. "Do you love me anymore?"

He stood alone, facing the strangely lit manor once more. The temperature dropped. His breath fogged. Static electricity raised the hair on his arms.

Hunter approached the oak door. Demons and angels ran rampant across the grain. Each figure followed him with grimacing stares, as though they knew something he didn't. When he looked away, the carvings seemed to breathe. When he looked back, they stilled. Lost in thought, he murmured, "The door of good and evil."

When he pressed the doorbell, a church bell chimed and refused to stop. Blood dripped from his nose. Still black. Two hours, twenty-seven minutes until alignment. The door hadn't opened. His hands trembled, they hadn't stopped trembling since the funeral. The chevrons screamed. His eyes watered uncontrollably. The world tilted three degrees.

He sprinted for the solarium tucked behind the house.

Hunter yanked a brick from the planter box. It struck with a loud boom, rattling the door's steel frame. A dog barked in the distance. When the world tilted again, his vision tunneled to black. That haunting whisper came clawing back, "There's no escaping us, Mr. Persefoni."

Two hours, twenty minutes.

When he woke, he could smell her sweetness. He found himself lying in the ballroom. Or had it been the conservatory? The ceiling stretched above him like alien shadows. The parquet floor smelled of fresh pine varnish. In the dark, he heard loafers prancing across wood. Those invisible soles rushed toward him, trampling over him. But no one was there. Eyes from the airport were upon him again. His watch read 3:39. It hadn't budged. The second hand twitched. Forward. Backward. Forward. That was all the proof he needed, he was no longer alone.

In the periphery, a figure emerged from the dark. It appeared evil, like a wild beast hunkered in the woods. Watching. Waiting. When he reached to touch it, laughter erupted from upstairs. The chevrons pulsed in rhythm with his racing heart.

A doorway glowed in the distance. As he moved toward it, another spell of laughter echoed from the end of the grand hall. He ignored the inviting light and went the opposite way.

Five minutes until alignment.

Fog rose from the floor. Not rolled in, but rose, from demolished foundations, from graves, from places fog had no business being. The air tasted coppery now. He was gaining traction.

He walked down the grand hallway, scrounging for signs of life. He stopped when familiar voices reached beyond time. When the door swung wide, there sat Mayer. Shadows slithered up the walls, mirroring flames from the fireplace.

The chevrons pulsed. Hunter blinked. The patterns stilled.

His watch still read 3:39.

He drew closer, covering his mouth. "Ember... Tara."

The television showed a date stamp in the corner: October 17, 2050. 3:33 p.m. That couldn't be right. They'd been dead for months. Or had it been weeks?

"They're here," Mayer said, glancing over Hunter's shoulder. "The ones your father warned me about."

That eerie feeling from the ballroom returned. "What did you do?" A haunting roar seized his throat as he reached for Mayer.

"They'll kill me."

"Tell him the truth, Mr. Kingsley," a woman said calmly. "This is your moment."

The chevrons pulsed. His eyes watered so badly he couldn't see.

"I—I'm sorry." Mayer stared, shaking his head.

With a sinister smile, Hunter gripped Mayer's neck and squeezed.

Four minutes until alignment.

Mayer didn't fight. He almost wished for death. His eyes sizzled red before his lids began to close. When he finally came to, Hunter stood over him, horrified. "What did I do?"

His watch read 3:39. Still 3:39. Blood dripped from his nose. Black blood pooled on the floor.

The woman laughed behind him. Or had she been laughing the entire time?

"Killing isn't your strong suit," she said. "Take a seat, Mr. Persefoni. There's room for one more."

"I don't—"

"What do you think is happening to you?"

The whispers weren't whispers anymore. The weave was pulling him somewhere he couldn't see yet.

"Let's fix this mess and be done with it, shall we?"

His brain started to shut down.

"You're quite the interesting fellow, Mr. Persefoni. I expected more." The woman laughed. Static noise persisted.

"Don't pat yourself on the back," Hunter said with a sluggish smirk. "You smell like shit."

"I will tell you something true." Those glowing eyes burrowed into him. "Three years from now, I ordered your family's removal. I don't know why yet."

"You... killed—"

With the sound of a pigeon coo, his body seized. No words could form.

A lighter sparked to life as she dragged the flame to her mouth. Her eyes glinted from the lit cigarette. When the ember flared, her eyes flared with it.

"I must have had a reason." She took another drag. "You're going to tell me why."

Her flawless skin, golden hair, and mirror eyes lent her a demon-child flare. But the woman was too perfect, nearly photoshopped.

She cooed again, his body reanimated. His watch still read 3:39. Black blood dripped from both nostrils now. Fear stirred within him. Her strange noises couldn't be overlooked. Hunter reached for explanations, a rare illness, maybe. What would cause a woman to sound like that?

She took another drag. Seconds later, smoke billowed. The mantle exploded with embers from a snubbed cigarette. Ashes floated down like falling stars. She calmly stepped into the light and removed the human suit.

Hunter sprawled back.

"You're becoming problematic, Mr. Persefoni," she said. "Just like the others."

Three minutes until alignment.

The woman inspected Hunter as though mildly intrigued by an insect. "You frighten us too, Mr. Persefoni."

"I doubt that." Hunter's throat caught.

"You already have the answers." Her voice, cold and sharp. The woman's throat vibrated and puffed out as she laughed with beastly appetite. "You don't know it yet."

"What's so funny?"

"You, Mr. Persefoni. You."

Hunter cleared his throat and tried to speak but paused when her skin slid off her frame. Beneath it, shimmering scales. The human suit struck him as robotic. "Your face. It's unraveling."

Within seconds, thick vapor swarmed. The strange smog emitted a miniature thunderstorm, synchronized and mechanical. "Aren't you curious?"

"I came for one thing." Hunter met Mayer's eyes.

"Poor Mr. Persefoni. You haven't pieced it together fast enough. You still think this is about you?"

"Enlighten me." He glared at the alien.

"You know, but you refuse to let us in."

He looked confused, like a child solving a puzzle without borders.

"You're a fixed coordinate now. This little family of yours is the key."

"You're crazy—"

Before Hunter could finish, his airway collapsed. He choked and gasped. The chevron exploded into instructions. Coordinates. A weave pulling him forward through time. His watch finally moved: 3:33. Black blood poured from his nose, his ears, his eyes. The woman smiled.

"The alignment approaches, Mr. Persefoni. Your daughter recognized it. That's why she had to die."

part three
the weave

"You will learn your place." She said it as static thickened the air and raised his hair. "Your entitlement is an illusion."

The cough infected his throat. He forced out a raspy word. "Okay."

"Your exact location before the crash?"

"I—I don't—" Hunter's eyes rolled white, and he sank to the floor coughing.

"The pain will never end. Not until we allow it."

That pigeon coo sliced the air, siphoning high, then low. The coughing spell vanished. He regained control.

"Who were you with?"

"I can't breathe—" Hunter stretched out his hand while an invisible noose tightened around his neck.

"Give us a name!"

He clawed at his throat.

"Think harder, Mr. Persefoni." Her voice, cold. "The timeline is eroding because of you."

Two minutes until alignment.

Hunter scanned the room for something to strike with. The creature wearing the human suit had no intention of letting him go. It played a better game than he did. Barbara's whereabouts weighed heavily on him the second he tasted death. In that moment, his well-devised plan reversed course. He no longer hated them. Barbara and Mayer must have been blackmailed by the creature. Now it had turned into a rescue mission.

Hunter had no idea where to start looking for Barbara. The glowing door at the end of the hall was a good start, but he needed to outsmart the creature. He could feel it snooping around inside his head, making a mess of things and screwing with his mind.

"James McDermott," he said. The first name that came to mind.

"Do you think I'm a fool, human?" She laughed and cooed those beastly sounds. "James McDermott is your ghost."

He sat there for a moment, running the idea through his mind over and over, searching for a reality that couldn't be ascertained. The more she laughed, the angrier he got. Something broke inside him.

Hunter sprang to his feet. The chair slid backward with Mayer in tow. He screamed. Grabbed the scotch bottle. Hurled it at the creature. His impulsive reaction took her by surprise. She didn't expect the incoming bottle until it was too late. Glass shattered. Liquor soaked the creature's fine wool.

Shards skipped across the brick, inches from the fire. Flames exploded as liquor splashed against the logs.

"We removed them from the temporal shift." The human suit melted away. Its eyes mirrored his frightened image. "We'll remove you too."

Hunter didn't allow the opportunity to slip and tossed the creature into the fireplace. It smashed against the chevron lining. Crumpled. Confused. Flames eagerly ate its pound of flesh. The creature howled as the fire consumed—a tea kettle exceeding boiling point.

Hunter stood there satisfied. His eyes mirrored the flames as he watched her burn.

"That's for them."

One minute until alignment.

Hunter checked on Mayer, only to realize he had died. He checked Mayer's pulse. Nothing. He pulled back his trembling finger. Who killed Mayer? Was it him? Or the creature? Or worse—maybe she fooled him into thinking Mayer was still alive, just to keep him talking.

Those awful noises kept playing inside his head, the gasping, the gurgling, and then the abrupt silence. The fireplace painted Mayer's somber face with a warm glow, those vacant eyes gazing at the ceiling.

He sprinted for that glowing door at the end of the corridor. The ghost of his daughter skated past him. The chevron whispers screamed coordinates. A weave pulled him forward. Toward something. Away from something. Time fractured.

Before entering the room, it was clear a scuffle had taken place. Objects strewn in the grand hall. Broken sconces. Shattered glass. Blood splattered the walls. Evidence of a struggle pained him more than the guilt.

Hunter entered the room undetected. The air was thick and uneasy. No signs of black static though. The creature claimed valuable real estate inside his head, which led him to believe more lurked in the dark corners. It had seemed far too easy to kill the creature. He'd worked harder at killing Mayer. His watch read 3:39. Or was it moving now? He couldn't tell. The second hand twitched. Stopped. Twitched.

Within seconds, he located Barbara. There, in the darkest corner, she was slumped over the sofa. Arms sprawled out. Frozen in a macabre swimmer's pose. She appeared to reach for something—that jeweled Rolex swimming in a sea of navy fabric like a twinkling star.

"Oh, God." His eyes blinded by tears. "What the fuck did they do to you?"

Propped nonchalant on the opposite side of the sofa was Barbara's decapitated head. Her facial expression was tired, frozen in mid-yawn. Blank gaze stuck on the ceiling. Hunter peered up, praying there was nothing to see. Black blood dripped from his nose. From his ears. From his eyes. The weave pulled tighter.

Tara and Barbara looked so much alike. Hunter got confused. Barbara's severed head kept flashing, Tara, then Barbara, then back to Tara. She mesmerized him. Haunted by what he could see. But the bizarre trance was sliced by a beastly coo. It rose from the dark. That dreaded sound grew and prickled his flesh.

Thirty seconds until alignment.

He sprinted to the grand staircase. Ghastly noises tightened all around him. An army of shadows clawed the walls, closing fist-like. They charged after him. He barreled toward the solarium door.

Each step brought faint relief. Once he hit the parquet floor, thunderous quakes vibrated the bottoms of his feet. The air around him suddenly carried a pulse, a static charge that climbed to the back of his throat. The chevrons started to scream. Coordinates shifting. Weaving. Unweaving.

As he burst into the ballroom, the alien horde had gained ground. He was no match. But somehow he meant to outlast. Live another day, only to kill again. He bolted through the solarium. His top half charged ahead like a locomotive. Something metal struck his face, but everything below kept moving.

Fifteen seconds until alignment.

The entire ordeal happened so fast the pain couldn't compute. A cold prickle filled his mouth—coppery. His face went numb. He lay there panting, fighting the urge to close his eyes. Above him, a sky full of stars. When he began to fade, a woman's voice rose.

"I'm intrigued, Mr. Persefoni." That iced tone slithered into his ears. "You're bleeding between when and when not."

"Don't you things die?" His voice gravel.

"Still having trouble piecing things together. We'll make the necessary corrections."

Fear and wonder filtered the air between them. The creature hovered over him, runway ready once again. Flawless hair, mirror eyes, the works. No blemishes. No superficial burns. Unscathed. Blocking his perfect view of the night sky.

"We never make the same error twice." She drew closer, that haunting coo locked in its throat.

"I'm coming back, and when I do—"

"I'm counting on it." She lifted the shovel high and smashed his face. She inspected him for a moment. "Blind to purpose, Mr. Persefoni. Aren't we all."

Black blood pooled beneath him. The chevrons no longer pulsed. Time fractured. The weave pulled him under.

Alignment.

Or was it?
His watch stopped. 3:33.

dark reality

Shadow figures stood watch from a distance, wearing the forest like a suit. The strange men from the San Francisco airport had followed Hunter to Kingsley Manor. Their clothing absorbed the woods—material that made them nearly invisible. They were outsiders from another world made to look like insiders, sent to observe. Mirror images of the ordinary world.

The October breeze carried pine sap and dew. Somewhere in the dark, an owl hooted, then fell silent, like a gentle heartbeat slowing toward death. Behind them, the manor's stone walls seemed to absorb the uneasiness in the air, as though drinking something they had tasted before. A single upstairs window went dark.

They watched the aliens stuff Hunter's body into the SUV. His limbs hung slack, head lolling against the doorframe. Black blood soaked through his shirt collar, catching the moonlight in an oily sheen. His wristwatch caught the light too, hands frozen at 3:33, though seconds earlier they had been spinning backward. Through the fabric of his sleeve, the chevron pulsed faintly—once, twice—then went dark.

The aliens grouped together near the rear bumper, standing in silence. They leaned toward one another, heads touching, as though synchronizing. Their pupils glowed with a pulse-like rhythm. Lips pursed, but their throats vibrated with a low coo that distorted the air.

One shadow glanced at his companion for confirmation, then turned his gaze back to the aliens. The other shadow reached out his hand, hesitating for just a heartbeat. Their chevrons beamed with dark matter, steady rather than pulsing. Time slowed with such clarity that everything around them froze in place. The owl hung mid-flight between branches. A single dewdrop suspended in its fall from a leaf. Even the October breeze died in the pines.

Dark matter oozed from their joined hands like poison, causing natural law to skirt outside the lines. The air around them rippled like summer heat, bending the fabric of time itself. Without words, they stepped sideways through reality. One burst of light, undetectable to the human eye. They vanished from the woods.

Where the shadow figures had stood, frost crept across the fallen leaves in geometric patterns. The dewdrop shattered against stone. Time resumed with a gasp, and the forest sounds flooded back instantly.

part four
marker one

No streetlight shone on Flying Point Road. The two-lane road clung to cold dreariness, its newly paved asphalt gleaming dully under scattered moonlight. October air bit at Lieutenant Williams's knuckles as he crouched near marker one, studying the body slumped against the oak tree.

The victim's position was impossible. The overturned vehicle sat at marker thirty-nine. Far too short a distance for ejection. Gasoline vapors mixed with wet leaves, a familiar cocktail from too many late-night calls. But the half bottle of Moët on marker five, still ice cold? That wasn't familiar. That was a message.

Williams's flashlight beam traced the victim's face. Male, mid-thirties, dark hair matted with blood. No identification. No fingerprints —the pads smooth as glass, as if they'd been lasered off. Another puzzle, the victim's hand. Strange geometric tattoos pulsed beneath the skin. Chevrons, angular and precise, glowing against pale flesh.

Williams had learned to trust his instincts young. They'd kept him alive in Harlem's foster system and guided him through thirteen years on the force. His adoptive father used to say the road to honor was measured in inches, not yards. Tonight felt like one of those inches.

He sat in the cruiser reviewing his notes, marking inconsistencies.

The scene tugged at his gut, but to the other officers, the case was already solved. Another drunk tourist who'd wrapped his car around a tree. John knew better.

Headlights raced down Flying Point Road from the opposite direction, exposing whatever the night wanted to keep hidden. The driver sped carelessly, swerving side to side. Tires squealed against pavement, making the road hum beneath spinning wheels.

Aliens didn't communicate as humans did. They conversed through cooing pitches and sixth sense, always traveling in groups of three. The Sovereign sat in the back seat, her blonde hair catching the dashboard lights. Behind her, stuffed into the cargo area like discarded luggage, lay Hunter. His shirt was soaked through with black blood that glistened like motor oil in passing headlights.

In unison, all three cooed a destructive vibrating pitch—not language, but ecstasy. The Sovereign fed on the terror ahead while her sentinels harmonized in anticipation. The pitch rattled the car windows. The driver pressed the gas pedal harder, forcing the vehicle to roar at top speed.

Once the SUV crested the hill, the aliens could see red and blue lights sweeping across the valley below. Strobe lights stretched and glistened against wet asphalt. The valley pulsed with artificial life.

One sentinel cooed another haunting pitch. The windows shuddered. The driver killed the headlights and smashed the gas pedal to the floor. The engine screamed. Wheels burned up asphalt. The vehicle shot down the peak like a bullet, steering erratically as the sentinel aimed for the lights below.

In the cargo area, Hunter's eyes snapped open. The chevrons burned—three sharp pulses against bone. His watch read 3:33. Then 3:34. Then 3:33 again. He tried to speak, but his mouth tasted like copper. Or oil. The blonde woman in the front seat turned to look at him, but her face rippled like water—features sliding off and reforming.

Two hours, eighteen minutes. Something whispered. Or did he say it? The voice felt like it came from inside his skull and outside the universe simultaneously. He couldn't remember closing his eyes.

Detective Spencer angled his cruiser across the road, blocking oncoming traffic. Another incident involving drugs and alcohol. Fatal car accidents had become routine in the Hamptons, inevitable as the morning tide.

"Got another, Sarge?" Spencer's voice echoed sharp.

Williams's eyes remained fixed on his notes. Without making eye contact, he said, "it's Lieutenant now."

"Damn, John, I didn't mean anything by it."

He closed the notebook. "Need your eyes on this."

"What spooked you?"

"Skid marks start at marker one, but marker thirty-nine dead-ends at the guardrail."

"What's the speed projection?" Spencer raised a brow.

"That's not even the strangest part. The body winds up on the double lines at marker one."

"Jesus Christ."

"The victim has no fingerprints. No identification, nothing. The vehicle doesn't even have a digital VIN. Everything was wiped clean." Williams paused, yanking something from his pocket. "This was next to the body."

He held up a gold wristwatch in an evidence bag. The face read 3:33. As Spencer stared at it, the second hand twitched backward, then forward, then stopped.

"The hell?" Spencer followed the watch as though it would run away.

Williams placed the gold watch to his ear. "Still ticking. But look at it."

They both watched as the minute hand spun counterclockwise, then snapped back to 3:33.

"Shit, John." Spencer canvased the wet road until it blurred into darkness.

"I found a half bottle of Moët on marker five, still ice cold. Like someone placed it there."

"I'll start at marker one."

John pocketed the watch. "You're not scared?"

Spencer locked eyes on the darkest parts of the road. "Bottle of Moët, gold watch, and a convertible. My money's on the wife."

"Or husband."

"Yeah." Spencer headed toward his cruiser under a spell. "Well, whoever it was must have a shit ton of money and a lot of connections."

"Whoever they are, we'll catch them."

He pulled an accident kit from the cruiser's trunk. While rummaging for flares and markers, a horrifying sound caused him to abandon his search. Spencer glared at the dark side of the hill. In the distance, he heard a vehicle racing toward the crime scene. Whoever was fast approaching had a bird's-eye view from the hilltop. With all the flares and strobing lights, how could anyone miss the accident?

Spencer yanked the gun from his hip. Flashlight in one hand, weapon in the other, he crisscrossed wrist over arm and aimed for the incoming vehicle.

"Something's coming!"

Williams heard panic rise in Spencer's throat and hit the asphalt running. They quickly formed a tactical position and moved up the road. Guns drawn, flashlights slicing through darkness, Spencer said, "Vehicle immobilizer?"

Williams shook his head. "I'll take the grass. You work the middle!"

Williams advanced up the side of the road while Spencer's boots pounded pavement. "I can't see a fucking thing!" Spencer bathed in the cruiser's strobe lights.

"Keep focus. When I tell you to shoot, you shoot!"

"Jesus..." The cruiser's strobe lights stung his eyes.

John advanced through tall grass, silent.

Spencer glared at Williams and yelled, "I got eyes on it!"

Hunter flickered to life. Voices outside. Human voices, shouting. His hand pulsed. The chevrons were screaming in frequencies he could taste. Light bled through his eyelids. He couldn't tell if his eyes were open. The watch—where was the watch? He'd been wearing it. Now it was gone. The hands had been spinning. Backward. Forward. Trapped.

Two hours, nine minutes. The whisper said. Blood dripped from his nose—black as ink in the darkness. Or red. His vision smeared colors together like wet paint.

The vehicle screeched to a clamorous halt. The tires kicked up a gigantic cloud of smoke. Burned rubber mingled in the beam of

Spencer's flashlight. The atmosphere electrified by the smell of rubber catching fire.

Eli aimed the flashlight at the SUV. Through the windshield, he could see the driver and front passenger clearly, two women with flawless features, luminous skin. Like starlets. "They're women, John."

"Women?"

"Fucking movie stars."

Williams squinted through the glare. He saw shapes, silhouettes, but their features kept shifting. One moment beautiful, the next monstrous, then back again. "Can't get a clear look."

They encircled the SUV, guns trained. Spencer inched closer. "Driver! Turn the vehicle off, right now!"

After years of experience, silence gave Williams the chills. Silence was always an introduction to something bad about to go down—especially the kind in which suspects hesitated, or worse, ignored an officer's command. When their commands fell on deaf ears, Williams knew the good guys always died first.

Williams put the assault rifle into go-mode, arming the sensor. "Turn off the vehicle, now!"

Inside the SUV, The Sovereign's pupils contracted to pinpoints. Something hummed beneath the chassis, a frequency undetectable to humans. The driver shined the car's high beams at Spencer. "Shit!"

The SUV's high beams caught his face, blowing out every shade until he looked like a phantom in the road.

"I see them. Two in the front and one in the back... move out of the light, Eli!" Williams inched closer and commanded, "Driver, show me some hands!"

"The driver's hands are still on the wheel!" Spencer said.

With an unnatural smile, The Sovereign took control of Spencer's mind. The aliens forced Spencer to point his weapon at Williams. His bulging brown eyes locked onto Williams. His mind scrambled beyond repair, brain stuttering between reels.

In Spencer's mind, John's face warped. Eyes too wide. Mouth full of static. The assault rifle in Williams's hands looked like a serpent, coiling, ready to strike. No, he screamed internally. *That's John. That's John. That's—*

But his trigger finger knew better. His finger knew the truth. His pants were soaked. When did that happen? The gun was so heavy. Or light. He couldn't feel his hands anymore.

Spencer battled the urge to shoot Williams. The gun quivered wildly in his grip.

"John, drop it, please, goddammit," Spencer pleaded.

Williams's brow furrowed, eyes darting between Spencer and the gun. "What the hell are you doing? Stand down!"

His pistol grip grew more violent as he walked toward Williams under a deep trance, as though he were a brain-eating zombie. "I can't control it."

Tears poured from his eyes unnaturally, high beams glinting off them like jewels. Lifeless expression amplified. As Spencer crossed paths with the headlights, Williams realized Spencer had pissed himself. By all appearances, his body was expelling every ounce of liquid it held. "I can't stop it... please... fucking shoot me, John, please—"

"Look at me, goddammit! It's me! It's me!" Williams begged.

The gun discharged and rocked the hillside with a final piercing call. The blast echoed hard against the dark desolation and scattered birds from nests. Crickets and owls remained indifferent, absorbing the single shot with their calls.

The aliens released Spencer's mind from their grip. His knees hit the wet pavement. He inspected the gun in his hand and flung it to the asphalt in disgust. He crawled to where Williams lay.

Williams struggled for life, Spencer beside him in the tall grass, clinging to his hand. Horrified to see all the damage he'd done. The bullet burned a hole in Williams's neck. Blood bubbled from the corner of his mouth.

He lay there, face stunned. Not anger. Not fear. Just bewilderment, like a child watching a magic trick he couldn't quite figure out. Williams choked, "You son of a bi—"

Williams had nothing left to give. The light from his eyes flickered out. Spencer began to cry and applied pressure to his neck. Those dead eyes burning a hole into his soul. "Fuck!"

The driver exited the vehicle and picked up the weapon lying on the road. She approached Spencer. He looked up. The alien towered over him, wearing a brilliant smile. With her voice ringing inside his head: *YOU STILL THINK THESE INSIGNIFICANT WEAPONS WILL SAVE YOUR LIFE, WHEN IN FACT, THEY ARE YOUR DOWNFALL.*

Spencer met her glowing eyes. "Fuck you, you piece of sh—"

A second gunshot stirred the valley. Sweet sounds of nature softened its percussion as the crickets sang from hiding one last time. Spencer swayed and fell forward, slumping over Williams.

Within seconds, she had dismantled the gun and tossed its guts onto the road. The aliens scanned the area, searching for living witnesses. She mounted the driver's seat and turned off the high beams.

The Sovereign: *Do share your meal.*

Her eyelids fluttered wildly and cast a blinding light. She stared at the road ahead, bathing the valley in white light. The aliens burst with a vibrating coo, as though feasting.

The Sovereign wiped her lips... *Scrumptious.*

The Sovereign suddenly screamed like a tea kettle and flailed in her seat. Her piercing call shattered the windows. With glowing eyes, the alien split apart like delicate crystal. Its human costume shriveled like burned plastic. Its albino scales glinted in the light. The sentinels looked at each other with fearful eyes. They didn't even make a sound before turning to ash.

Shadow figures crept from the woods with a sense of urgency. One placed a crystal on the SUV's hood. The device hummed below human frequency—but not below Ouroboros perception.

"Did we arrive in time?" The shadow figures' clothing mirrored the wet asphalt.

"He's alive."

"What about them?" He pointed at Williams and Spencer, lying dead in the tall grass.

"We don't interfere with the loop. The officers would have died either way. Deliver the chosen one to the Synods. I'll take care of the rest."

The shadow figure opened the hatch, placed Hunter over his shoulders, and said, "I hope he's everything they say he is."

"The Synods have already seen the outcome. He will remove the Time Keeper."

"I hope they're right, brother. Humans must evolve naturally, as their ancestors once did."

"If we do nothing, then there will be nothing."

"Maybe that's the point." He activated the crystal device and vanished with Hunter.

The SUV began to rock back and forth wickedly. Its lights flashing. Horn screaming. The ground remained calm as the vehicle twisted and buckled. Metal crunching over metal. Glass singing. In an instant, the SUV balled up like scrap paper. It smashed together so tightly that it vanished.

The shadow figure went to the dead officers and touched Williams's wound, then placed a finger on Spencer. Each hole pulsed with blue light. The piercing glow quickly infected their circulatory systems, electrifying each cell. Their skin tracing blue pathways everywhere.

Within seconds, the blue light burned out and Spencer woke. Renewed vitality pulsed through him.

The October wind had picked up, carrying the smell of burnt rubber and something else—ozone, maybe. Or lightning. He didn't care. Williams's blood was cooling under his hands. How long had they been partners? Eight years? Ten? He couldn't remember, couldn't think. I killed him. I killed him. The words looped in his mind like a scratched record.

Somewhere behind him, metal groaned, and then hands touched his shoulders. The shadow figure towered over him like a strange wonder. Spencer didn't believe in a higher power, but now he was convinced something unexplainable existed .

As John reanimated, the shadow figure said, "Your friend is vital. Use this gift wisely."

An endless cough locked Williams's throat, as if a bullet were still lodged.

Spencer turned to gaze upon the shadow figure, only to realize he had vanished. All there was left to see was a rising sun—too red, too fast, like something was rushing time forward.

"You shot me, you son of a bitch!" Williams flailed in the tall grass.

With overwhelming emotion, Spencer plopped down on the grass. "I never thought it would go down like this. Not like this."

John coughed more. He touched his neck. Smooth skin. No scar. No proof.

"Did that just—" Williams started.

"Don't," Spencer said. "Just don't."

John staggered to his feet and looked toward marker one. The body against the tree, the John Doe with no fingerprints, the strange chevron tattoos, was gone. Just bark and leaves.

Spencer followed his gaze. The oak tree stood alone in the dawn light. No victim. No evidence.

The two sat there, side by side in silence, taking in whatever there was left to see. In the grass beside them, frost crept in geometric patterns, even though it was October, even though the temperature was rising.

John pulled the evidence bag from his pocket. The watch inside still read 3:33. As they stared at it, the second hand twitched backward, then forward, then stopped.

Neither of them said a word.

part five
space for eden

Hunter's eyes snapped open. Metal ceiling. Starlight shimmer above. Wrong. All wrong. The chevrons on his hand pulsed. Three sharp beats, then bone rattle. His watch read 3:33. Still. Always.

Seven hours. Something whispered.

He sat up too fast, head spinning. The glass garden. The blonde woman. Blackout. Nothing between then and now. Just a void where his hyperthymesia-prone brain should be recording everything. His body ached, but underneath the pain, something else thrummed. Raw energy. Youthful vitality he hadn't felt since boyhood. Like he could fly. Like he could bench-press a thousand cars. Like something was very, very wrong.

Classical music screeched from hidden speakers, butchered by distortion. Each note stabbed at his skull. Hunter sprang up, blood dripped from his nose. He wiped it. Black. He blinked. Red. The chevrons pulsed again. The air tasted coppery. Ozone before a lightning storm.

In the darkness, someone was watching. A woman sat motionless in the shadows, young, impossibly young, but her eyes were ancient. Eyes that seemed to glow in the low light.

"Where am I?" Hunter's voice cracked.

"You're among friends," the woman said.

The chamber pulsed like stars trapped in metal. Every surface absorbed sound. Elements not on any periodic table. It felt wrong. Too perfect. Too comfortable. Even the air was neither hot nor cold, perfectly neutral, perfectly sterile.

A seamless porthole cast light into his pod. Shadows interrupted the beam, swaying and flickering, dark silhouettes that moved like nothing human.

His breath quickened. "Aliens?"

"You're safe." Her voice was childlike but bore something ancient. "For now."

Hunter glared at the woman. "More games."

"I'm Arlowe." She stepped into the porthole's light, its pale glow penciling the edges of her face. Sun-kissed skin. Fiery hair. Nearly human. But those eyes—those impossible green eyes—dragged a chill through him. She could've passed for a teenager if not for the voice that followed, low and steady, carrying the weight of centuries. "The shadow figures pulled you from Kingsley Manor before the weave collapsed."

Four hours, twelve minutes.

Hunter held his head, reached out to steady himself. "You were supposed to save—"

Arlowe moved toward him slowly, hands visible. "You're confused. The temporal displacement affects memory formation."

"She didn't die—" Hunter stopped. His nose was bleeding again. He wiped it. Black blood smeared across his hand. He blinked. Red blood. The copper taste intensified. "What's happening to me?"

"The weave is opening. Your body is caught between all timelines, fixed and unfixed. You're becoming unstuck."

Hunter stared at his hand. The chevrons weren't just tattoos or pulses anymore. They shifted, rearranging into new configurations. Or had they always looked like that? He couldn't remember.

"You killed my daughter," Hunter said flatly.

Arlowe's expression didn't change. "No. The woman at Kingsley Manor did."

"Bullshit!"

"You're still alive." Arlowe gestured to the chamber. "If we wanted you dead, you'd be dead. You have something they fear."

"Fear." He stumbled, catching himself. "They could end me like that."

"You and Ember can manipulate timeline convergence. You see the weave. If you can see it, you can change it. That's why your watch won't work. That's why the chevrons chose your hand."

Hunter looked down at his wrist. The watch was there. Then it wasn't. Then it was again—hands spinning backward, then forward, then both directions at once.

"That's why you can kill Ouroboros." Arlowe's eyes met his. "You see multiple fixed points before they can."

"I didn't kill them. They just... died."

"No. You destabilized their temporal anchor. Ouroboros exist across multiple timelines simultaneously—that's their strength. But you collapse those timelines. Force them into a single moment. Make them mortal."

Hunter's chest tightened. "Ember?"

"She's stronger. That's why they got to her first."

The room tilted. Hunter grabbed the wall for support. The alloy felt like snakeskin. Smooth scales that slithered beneath his palm, responding to his touch with barely perceptible movement. Neither hot nor cold. Just alive.

"Can I bring her back?" Hunter said through gritted teeth.

Arlowe flickered. For just a moment, she wasn't there. Then she was. Her outline wavered like heat distortion. But Hunter could still sense her. She was there. Not there. Everywhere. All at once.

"Help us," she said. "She's waiting."

"Who's waiting?"

"The Arcanum." Arlowe flickered again, her voice layering over itself. "She'll show you what you need to see."

Hunter blinked hard. The ozone smell intensified. Lightning without thunder. "Show me what?"

"The choice you already made."

The alloy liquefied and evaporated like steam as they passed through the porthole. Hunter stepped into the Dall—a city of stars and impossible geometry stretching into darkness. Wherever his eyes landed, surfaces glowed with alien luminescence. The air hummed with a frequency just below hearing, vibrating in his skull.

Hunter's skin crawled. The Dall felt like it had been designed by something that studied beauty but didn't quite understand it. Every surface too smooth. Every angle too perfect. The silence was absolute except for that subsonic hum that rattled bone.

"What is this place?" Hunter whispered.

"The first human civilization."

"We're on Earth?" Hunter stopped. "Before Mesopotamia? Before—"

"Before everything you know." Arlowe's voice carried no pride, only fact. "The alloy and technology are from another place. A ninth planet just beyond the outer region of our solar system."

Hunter glided his fingers over the alloy. It responded to his touch, warming slightly, then cooling, then settling back to neutral. Scales slithered beneath his fingertips. The surface glowed with each step, like the Dall itself was alive. Watching. Guiding.

The chevrons on his hand screamed. He gasped and pulled away. The air crackled with ozone.

Six hours.

The countdown had restarted. Hunter's breath caught. He'd been here before. Was here now. Would be here again. All at once.

The Dall gradually darkened. Its shimmer faded, replaced by something insidious. Hunter felt an evil presence lurking ahead. Multiple pods rose from the dark, bathed in purple light that pulsed like a heartbeat.

A strange voice whispered inside his head: *Pass with caution.*

But curiosity pulled him forward. He reached for the door, hypnotized by its pulse. The chevrons on his hand flared white-hot.

"Stop!"

Hunter lowered his hand slowly. "Something told me not to. But I did it anyway."

"Ouroboros are on the other side. Remember that woman at Kingsley Manor?" Arlowe said sharply. "They won't hesitate."

Hunter stared at the glowing door. The whispers intensified. Not words, but frequency. A vibration that bypassed his ears and went straight to his nervous system. Fear. Rage. Hunger. The taste of copper flooded his mouth again.

"They're afraid," Hunter whispered.

Arlowe's face remained impassive. "Good."

"How can you justify keeping them here?"

"They murdered people for breakfast, including people like your daughter." Arlowe's eyes hardened. "Would you prefer we release them?"

Hunter said nothing. The chevrons pulsed once, twice. The Ouroboros on the other side could sense him. And he could sense them, trapped and suffering. She was right. He knew she was right. But knowing didn't make it easier.

"They killed Ember," Hunter said quietly. "But they're still—"

"Don't." Arlowe warned. "Don't humanize them."

They continued down the corridor, but the whispers from behind the door lingered in his mind.

The world went white.

Hunter gasped. Ozone filled his lungs. He was walking. Had been walking. How long? Arlowe flickered beside him. There, not there, still there in the spaces between moments. Time had skipped. Minutes? Hours? He was living it all simultaneously.

Three hours, forty-one minutes.

"What—" Hunter stumbled.

"You're fragmenting," Arlowe said. Her voice sounded far away. "We're almost there."

The alien corridor opened into an enormous city. A waterfall cascaded through the center, frozen mid-fall. No, moving so slowly it only seemed frozen. Hunter's head throbbed. The copper taste was overwhelming now.

"Why does this place feel wrong?" Hunter asked.

"Because it is." Arlowe flickered again. "We must pass through the detention wing."

The pods here were smaller, reinforced, bathed in that same purple light. Behind each door, he could feel things watching. His chevrons pulsed in rhythm with his footsteps now. Each beat sending a jolt through his nervous system.

"How many are there?" Hunter whispered.

"Enough." Arlowe's outline wavered. "We've been capturing them for millennia."

"And if they escape?"

"They won't."

But her voice carried doubt. Just a trace, but enough for Hunter to notice across all the timelines where she said it.

Another white flash. Ozone. Lightning. Hunter blinked. He was standing in a massive dome-shaped chamber. When had they arrived? The shell pulsed with layers of overlapping light. The alloy here felt different, warmer, almost organic. Scales that breathed.

An apprentice sat behind a large floating desk, smiling. Hunter's heart stopped.

Those eyes.

"Ember?" he whispered.

Her smile widened. "Not exactly. But close enough."

One hour, fifty-seven minutes.

"You're not real."

"Does it matter?" She gestured to a seat that hadn't been there a moment ago. "The Arcanum is rising."

Hunter looked for Arlowe. She flickered in and out of existence now, more absent than present. But he could feel her. She was still there. Still watching. Always watching.

"What is this?"

"The Arcanum exists everywhere," the apprentice said. Her voice layered, overlapping. "She must collapse, to meet you. Sometimes that means wearing a familiar face."

Hunter turned back. The girl wore Ember's smile. Ember's eyes. "Should I be scared?"

The apprentice's smile didn't reach her eyes. "She'll show you what you want to see, Hunter." She paused. "Not what's true."

Hunter's blood went cold. "What does that mean?"

"It means," she said softly, "truth and desire aren't always the same thing. And the Arcanum knows which one you'll choose."

"Where is she?"

"Behind you." The apprentice's smile widened impossibly. Then she liquefied, pooling on the desk before evaporating into mist.

Hunter froze. The chevrons burned white-hot. The perimeter wall had vanished. What took its place was a never-ending abyss. Not darkness, movement. Shapes forming and reforming in the void. The smell of ozone was suffocating.

COME CLOSER. The voice came from everywhere and nowhere. Familiar. Impossibly familiar.

He stepped toward the abyss. The floor beneath him rippled like water but held solid. Snakeskin scales slithering beneath his feet.

"Look at me."

He looked up.

The Arcanum stood before him. She was—

"It can't be." Hunter's breath caught. "Mom?"

His mother smiled, but her face kept shifting. His mother, then Tara, then Ember, then all three at once, then someone else entirely. A face he'd never seen but somehow recognized across every timeline.

"This isn't real," Hunter whispered.

"Does real matter?" The Arcanum touched his chest, over his racing heart. "You're the fixed point, Hunter. You choose what survives."

The chevrons erupted across his body, covering his neck, his face, spreading like living circuitry. He could feel them burrowing deeper, fusing with bone, with blood, with soul.

"Don't ask me to choose," Hunter said, tears streaming. "I can't—"

"You already did."

The moment her hand pressed harder, reality shattered. The air crackled with lightning. Ozone flooded his senses.

Forty-seven minutes.

Hunter saw it all. The car crash branching into infinite possibilities. In one timeline they survived. In another, he died instead. In another, they never got in the car. In another, Ember was never born. He was living every single one.

The glass garden at Kingsley Manor. Ouroboros attacking. In one timeline he killed them all. In another, they killed him. In another, the shadow figures arrived sooner. All happening at once.

Flying Point Road. John and Eli dying, resurrecting, dying again, never dying. His body at marker one. His body in the SUV. His body was nowhere at all. Every possibility branching into infinite timelines. All colliding, all converging, all screaming toward a single point through him.

Him.

"The weave is opening," the Arcanum said. Her voice was his mother's, Tara's, Ember's. All speaking in perfect harmony. "When the portal opens, only one reality survives."

"How?" Hunter gasped. Blood poured from his nose. Black and red mixed together. The copper taste was choking him.

"Let go."

The Arcanum pressed harder. Hunter screamed as the chevrons ignited, white-hot and blinding.

His watch shattered. The hands spun wildly before flying off entirely. Three-thirty-three dissolved into meaningless numbers. But Hunter could feel the watch in other timelines, whole, broken, never existing at all.

"I want them back," Hunter sobbed. "Tara. Ember. I just want them back."

"Then choose the timeline where they live."

Hunter's mind reeled. He saw it. The timeline where Tara and Ember survived the crash. Where they were home right now, safe, laughing, alive.

"Show me," he whispered.

The Arcanum gestured. The abyss parted.

Hunter saw his kitchen. Tara making coffee. Ember at the table, doing homework, complaining about algebra. Alive. Safe. Happy.

"But I die in that one," Hunter said.

"Yes."

Hunter stared at the vision. Tara looked up, as if sensing something. For just a moment, her eyes met his across every timeline they'd ever shared.

"Will she know?" Hunter asked, his voice breaking. "Will they remember me?"

"You'll be the whisper where a person should have been."

Hunter's breath shook. "So I just... disappear?"

The Arcanum's eyes, all three faces at once, softened. "You become what they feel but can't name."

Twenty-nine minutes.

Hunter thought about all the years he'd wasted chasing money, power, validation. All the time he could have spent with Ember. All the moments with Tara he'd taken for granted. He thought about his father. About the cycle of damage passed down.

About breaking it.

"What if I can't?" Hunter whispered.

The Arcanum's grip tightened. "You can. You will."

"Will it hurt?"

"Yes," she said. "But not for long."

Hunter looked at his hands. The chevrons covered every inch of skin now, pulsing with white light. He was becoming the weave itself. The space between moments. The fixed point where all timelines converged.

Twelve minutes.

Hunter almost pulled away. His hand twitched. The Arcanum's eyes flashed, all three faces watching him with infinite patience.

"I'm afraid."

"I know."

"There must be another way."

The Arcanum spoke without words.

Eight minutes.

Hunter closed his eyes. Saw Tara's face one last time. Ember's laugh. Every moment he'd ever spent with them across every timeline. Then he saw himself fading, dissolving, becoming nothing. Not even a memory.

Just absence.

"Tell Ember I love her," Hunter said. "Even if she doesn't remember me."

"She'll feel it," the Arcanum said softly. "In dreams. In the spaces between whispers."

Hunter opened his eyes. Smiled through tears. "I know what I must do now."

The Arcanum nodded. "You always did."

The chevrons consumed him entirely. Hunter became light, became pattern, became the weave itself. Ozone filled the air, crackling with electricity.

"Thank you," he whispered.

Three minutes.

The portal opened. Reality split. Every timeline converged.

Hunter felt himself tearing apart, physically, temporally. His consciousness fragmenting across timelines, stretching impossibly thin. He could feel Arlowe watching from other fixed points. Could feel John and Eli in their patrol car. Could feel Tara and Ember sleeping in the timeline where they lived.

One minute.

He saw Tara laughing in their kitchen. Ember opening Christmas presents. John and Eli alive, patrolling Flying Point Road on a quiet night.

He saw himself fading. Dissolving. Becoming the space between nothing.

The alignment completed.

Hunter smiled.

Thirty seconds.

The Dall exploded with light.

Fifteen seconds.

Hunter let go.

Ten.

The waterfall froze.

Five.

The sky split open.

Four.

The chevrons went dark.

Three.

The ozone smell dissipated.

Two.

The copper taste faded.

One.

Hunter Persefoni disappeared.

Silence.

Tara Kingsley woke gasping for air.

Six hours.

The whisper came from nowhere. From everywhere. She sat up, heart pounding. Beside her, Ember stirred in her sleep, murmuring something about Christmas lights. Outside, the sun rose over a quiet neighborhood. No car crash. No glass garden. No Ouroboros. Just another Tuesday morning in a timeline that almost wasn't.

She touched her chest, right over her heart. For just a moment, she felt something, like someone watching over her. Like someone letting go. The air tasted faintly of copper. Like ozone before a storm.

She shook her head and went to make coffee, the feeling already fading. But warmth lingered. Unexplained. Comforting.

Five hours, forty-one minutes.

In her daughter's room, Ember dreamed of a man with kind eyes and strange marks covering his skin, telling her everything would be okay. When she woke, she wouldn't remember his face. But she'd remember the feeling. Safe. Loved. Protected.

Five hours, twelve minutes.

And on Flying Point Road, Lieutenant John Williams sat in his cruiser, staring at a wristwatch he'd found at marker one, a crime scene that didn't exist in any report. The hands were frozen at 3:33. The metal felt warm in his palm, almost alive. Like snakeskin.

He pocketed the watch and drove on, unaware that somewhere, in the space between fixed points, a man named Hunter Persefoni had saved them all.

Unaware that the countdown had begun again.

Four hours, fifty-seven minutes.

part six
creature inside

Arlowe stood at the edge of the abyss, watching. Hunter Persefoni's body had hung motionless in the void for three weeks, six days, and nine hours. Suspended in the space between timelines, caught in the Arcanum's grip.

The chevrons covering his skin pulsed erratically—white, then gold, then alien colors. Each pulse sent ripples through reality itself. The air in the dome tasted coppery, like ozone before a storm.

Beside her, the woman with Ember's eyes stood perfectly still, hands clenched. She hadn't moved in hours. Hadn't spoken. Just watched her father die and resurrect and die again across infinite timelines.

"How much longer?" the girl whispered.

Arlowe didn't answer. She didn't know.

The Arcanum had taken Hunter into the weave twenty-three days ago. For him, only minutes had passed. But in the Dall's linear time, they had been waiting. Praying he'd survive what no one else had—the Epicarp, a moment in time when all timelines converged into a single point. The moment when the fixed point either stabilized or shattered completely.

No human had ever survived the Epicarp. Their consciousness

fragmented across too many realities, unable to anchor to any single one. They became ghosts of nothing. But Hunter was different. He'd been living multiple timelines simultaneously since the moment the chevrons chose him. The weave had been preparing him for this.

"He's coming back," Arlowe said quietly.

The girl's head snapped up. "How do you know?"

"Because the countdown stopped."

In the void, Hunter's body convulsed. The chevrons erupted across every inch of skin, blazing white-hot. His mouth opened in a silent scream that rippled through dimensions.

The Arcanum released him.

Hunter fell.

Arlowe caught him before he hit the floor, his weight nearly taking her down. The girl—Ember—rushed forward, hands shaking as she reached for her father's face.

"Daddy?" she whispered.

Hunter's eyes were closed. Blood dripped from his nose—black, then red, then black again. The chevrons covering his body flickered like dying stars.

"Is he—" Ember's voice broke.

"He's breathing," Arlowe said. "But barely."

His chest rose and fell in shallow gasps. His skin was too cold. They lowered him to the floor. The alloy beneath him rippled, responding to his presence. Snakeskin scales slithered, adjusting, trying to stabilize him.

"Hunter." Arlowe forced his eyes open. "Stay with us. You made it through."

Ember pressed her hands to his chest, tears streaming. "Please don't leave me. Not again."

For a long moment, nothing. The dome held its breath. Even the alloy beneath them stilled.

Then his eyes snapped open.

The chevrons across his body blazed once, synchronized, then went dark. Only his eyes remained lit.

They glowed with impossible light—gold, silver, white, nameless colors that shouldn't exist in any spectrum. His pupils were gone, replaced by shifting patterns that looked like the chevrons themselves.

His hand twitched. Fingers curled into fists, then released, as if testing whether they still belonged to him.

Ember gasped and pulled back. "Is he one of them?"

"Hunter?" Arlowe whispered.

He sat up mechanically, as if learning how to move his body for the first time. His head turned toward them with unnatural precision. When he spoke, his voice was layered—dozens of overlapping echoes speaking in perfect unison.

"Hunter's not here anymore."

Arlowe's blood went cold. "Who are you?"

"The fixed point. The anchor." He looked down at his hands. The chevrons had stopped spreading, frozen in their final pattern. "I'm everywhere now. Every possibility. All at once."

He stood. The movement was fluid but wrong—too graceful, too controlled, like something that had studied how humans moved but wasn't quite one anymore.

Ember scrambled backward, terrified. "Dad?"

The thing wearing Hunter's face turned to her. For just a moment, something flickered in those glowing eyes, recognition. Then it was gone.

I'm sorry, baby. A single voice whispered beneath the others.

Hunter's voice, raw and breaking. "I had to choose. I chose you."

Ember's face crumpled. She lunged forward, wrapping her arms around him. "I don't want you to go."

What was left of him held her stiffly, as if he'd forgotten how to love. As if the memory of holding his daughter existed across too many timelines to access just one.

"I know," he said. The layered voices softened. "But I had to. So you could live."

Arlowe watched, her throat tight. She'd seen the Epicarp destroy dozens of people, watched them fracture and dissolve. But she'd never seen someone survive it and become something else entirely.

Hunter pulled back from Ember, looking down at her with those alien eyes. In their glow, Arlowe could see reflections—not this moment but infinite others. Ember at eight years old. At sixteen. At three.

Unborn. Dying. Every version of her that ever was or could be. All because he'd chosen her.

"How long was I gone?" Hunter asked. His voice was still layered but more controlled now. More focused.

"Three weeks, six days, nine hours," Arlowe said.

Hunter blinked. The glow in his eyes flickered. "I was only in there for—" He stopped. "Minutes. I experienced minutes."

"Time moves differently in the weave," Arlowe said. "You know that now. You exist in all of them."

Hunter looked at his hands again, turned them over. The chevrons pulsed with each heartbeat—if he even had a heartbeat anymore. "I can feel them," he whispered. "Every timeline. Every choice. Every consequence."

"Can you control it?"

Hunter's head tilted. "I am it."

Arlowe stepped closer, studying him. "You survived the Epicarp. No one survives—"

"Hunter didn't survive." His glowing eyes met hers, and Arlowe saw her own reflection multiplied across infinite realities. "He became something else. Something the Ouroboros can't kill."

He turned toward the dome's exit. "Take me to the prisoners."

Arlowe's eyes widened. "The detention wing? Why?"

"Because one of them knows where the device is." Hunter's voice was flat, absolute. "The one who killed me at Kingsley Manor. They have the coordinates."

"They'll never cooperate."

"They will. I can do what they do. I can see their timelines. Collapse them. Make them mortal." He paused. "Erase them."

Arlowe felt ice crawl up her spine. They'd wanted a weapon. They'd gotten one. But weapons didn't always obey their makers.

"And when you have the device?" Arlowe asked quietly.

"I align the worlds. I retrieve what was taken. I start the war."

Ember stood, wiping tears. "What did they do to you?"

Hunter turned back to her one last time. The glow in his eyes dimmed. He looked almost human.

"I don't know, baby. I'm still figuring out what I am." His voice cracked—just Hunter's, no layers. "But I need you to do something for me."

Ember nodded.

"In the timeline where your mother is alive, where you're both safe." His glowing eyes reflected her tear-streaked face across infinite possibilities. "Tell her I love her. Tell her I'm watching over you both."

Ember nodded, unable to speak.

Hunter reached out and touched her face. His hand was cold. The chevrons on his palm pulsed against her skin.

"You're so beautiful," he whispered. "So much like your mom."

Ember's lips trembled. She wanted to memorize this moment—his face, his voice, even the cold touch of his hand. But already he was pulling away.

Then he turned toward the exit.

"Hunter," Arlowe called. "What if you can't come back? What if the device—"

"I'm already everywhere, Arlowe." Hunter looked back at her with those terrible, glowing eyes. "There's no coming back from that. There's only moving forward."

He stepped through the dome, the alloy liquefying around him like water—and was gone.

Into the detention wing.

Into the war.

Into everything that came next.

Arlowe and Ember stood in silence, staring at the empty doorway.

"Is he still my father?" Ember whispered.

Arlowe's jaw tightened. "Not anymore."

But she hoped the girl was right.

From somewhere deep in the Dall, a sound echoed—not quite a scream, not quite a roar. The sound of something ancient and powerful recognizing a threat.

The Ouroboros had felt him coming.

Ember touched her chest, right where Hunter had held her. The warmth of his hand was already fading, but something else remained—a presence, like someone watching over her.

"He's still there," Ember said softly. "Somewhere. He's still my dad."

Arlowe said nothing. She'd seen too much to be certain.

In the distance, purple light pulsed from the detention wing. Then it went dark.

Whisper of war had begun.

part seven
human apple

Hunter's eyes snapped open, flickering like a moth trapped in a jar.

"Four months," a voice echoed.

He jerked upright. Arlowe stood in the doorway, older and harder than he remembered. Scars crossed her arms in geometric patterns that mirrored his own. "You've been in stasis. Your body needed time to integrate the transformation." She stepped closer. "Fixed points don't survive the Epicarp."

Hunter looked down at his hands. The chevrons moved beneath his skin, circuitry rearranging itself with each breath.

"Four months?" His voice was unsteady. "How—"

"Three weeks inside the Epicarp. Four months in medical stasis while your body adapted." Arlowe's voice softened. "Nearly five months. I'm sorry, Hunter."

Tara and Ember had been dead for almost half a year. He waited for the grief to come, searched for it inside the empty cavity where his heart used to pound. Nothing had survived the accident except that steady, mechanical rhythm. Thirty beats per minute. Like a clock winding down.

"Ember," he said, his eyes canvassing the room. "Is she—"

"Back in her timeline. The one you chose." Arlowe paused. "She doesn't remember you, Hunter. No one in that timeline does."

Her words should have hit like a bullet, but his pulse stayed steady. No glimmer of pride in his eyes. His daughter was safe, for now. "The device," he said. "Where is it?"

Before Arlowe could answer, the room flashed bright red. An alarm rattled from above. Hunter slid from the bed and hit the floor. Sickness rose fast. His throat convulsed. Black bile erupted from his mouth, spattering the sterile floor. It hissed—actually hissed—like acid eating through metal.

Two bots emerged and hesitated, their lights flickering erratically. They absorbed the substance and zipped away faster than usual. Hunter stared at the spot where the glowing bile had been. "What the fuck is happening to me?"

"Your body is rejecting its humanity," Arlowe said without emotion. "Or maybe it's the other way around."

A laser swept across his body, then several spheres rose and burst on contact, liquid absorbing into his skin. Within seconds, black fabric covered him.

"Neural-adaptive," Arlowe said. "Temperature regulation, injury monitoring. Ouroboros can't read your mind while you're wearing it."

His reflection caught in a nearby surface. His eyes glowed faintly— gold, silver, white. And he wasn't blinking.

"Come," Arlowe said, noticing. Her face paled. "You need to eat."

In the monumental expanse, plant life hung suspended along walls like thick green hair. The mess hall stretched below, packed with people —groups so diverse it astonished him. Pleasant aromas tempted his appetite. People sat eating peacefully, together.

Hunter felt something crack inside his chest. "This could never be us," he said quietly. "Our world would choose death."

"We've had more practice," Arlowe said.

Hunter watched a child laugh, pulling at her mother's sleeve. Another family across the hall—different skin, different language— smiled at them.

The chevrons pulsed brighter. People at nearby tables noticed. Went quiet. Backed away.

They could sense what he was. A child started crying, pointing at him. The mother scooped her up and fled, the child's scream echoing in the vast hall long after they'd departed.

Hunter waited for the instinct to comfort her, to apologize, to feel anything. His face remained blank. The chevrons pulsed brighter. And in that moment, he understood: the child wasn't wrong to be afraid. She'd recognized the monster before he had.

"Get me food," Hunter said. "Then take me to them."

There was no need to explain. Arlowe understood. Hunter's next stop would be Ouroboros.

Hunter took a seat at an empty table. The stool adjusted automatically. As soon as he sat, people at neighboring tables stood and moved farther away. The isolation was absolute.

A drone delivered a tray. Hunter stared at the burger—immaculate, almost fake. But the smell removed all apprehension. He snatched it up and tore off a massive chunk. Flavors exploded.

He forced himself to blink. It took effort, like his body was forgetting how. He looked down at what he was eating. The patty looked like freshly excavated worms—translucent strands with ribbed textures. Hunter stopped chewing. Spit everything out. No disgust. No emotion. Just mechanical rejection. His body made the decision without consulting him first.

"Worms," a voice said behind him. "That was my first thought too."

The boy hovered over his table, grinning. Unlike everyone else, he didn't look afraid. Just curious. "You see those long, stringy plants up there? That's these little guys. I'm Kade."

Hunter shook his hand as though he'd recognized the boy. "Hunter."

Kade waved away the small crowd that had gathered. "Nothing to see here, folks. The worm sandwich strikes again."

People dispersed but kept their eyes on them. Kade sat across from Hunter—a bold move, considering everyone else had fled. "First day of summer camp?"

"Something like that."

"I remember mine. Seven years ago. Sixteen and bleeding from a gunshot wound, convinced I was dying." Kade laughed, lightly hammering the table with his fist. "Shadow figures pulled me out right before Ouroboros found me."

Hunter studied the kid. Saw himself twenty years ago—angry, righteous, convinced he could change the world. "Why would Ouroboros want you?"

Kade's smile faded. "I blow stuff up."

Hunter's eyes widened. "Oh my God. You're that kid. The Pentagon."

"Yeah." Kade's expression darkened. "Sixteen screams naivety. Thought I could wake people up. Evacuated the building first—fire alarms, automated warnings. No one died." He laughed bitterly. "But it didn't matter. Within a week, half the country thought it never happened. The other half thought it was justified. I didn't wake anyone up. I just gave them another reason to fight."

Hunter felt something stir. Not grief. Not empathy. Just recognition. This kid had lost everything too. The chevrons on Hunter's body pulsed. Kade noticed but didn't comment.

"You're different," Kade said quietly. "Everyone here is different, but you—there's something else."

"I'm a fixed point," Hunter said. "I exist across multiple timelines."

"That's why they're afraid."

"You don't want this jackpot, kid."

An uncomfortable silence fell. Kade broke it. "Hey, you want to see something mind-blowingly weird?"

Hunter hesitated, then nodded.

"Request an apple. You're gonna need it until you get used to rabbit food."

A drone delivered an apple—red and perfect, like something from Eden.

Hunter bit into it. The flesh was sweet, crisp, but wrong. A metallic bitterness flooded his mouth, coating his tongue like copper pennies in honey.

Kade led Hunter to an observation deck. Through massive portholes, Hunter could see an alien forest outside—towering trees with shimmering bark. Two suns hanging low in a sky that was the wrong shade of blue.

"This isn't Earth." Hunter's voice still lacked emotion.

"Yes and no. The Dall exists in a pocket dimension, anchored to Earth but separate. That forest is Earth as it was three hundred thousand years ago. Before humans evolved." Kade leaned against the porthole. "The Synods built this place to preserve what Earth could be."

Hunter watched children playing below in a courtyard, laughing, chasing each other. Then he noticed their parents—shoulders tense, hands never far from their children, eyes scanning. Because even here, they knew the truth. Ouroboros was out there, hunting.

Hunter watched a mother pull her daughter close, whisper something in her ear. The girl nodded solemnly—too solemn for a child. She'd been taught to fear. Just like Ember had been.

Hunter looked at the apple in his hand. He was squeezing it too hard. The flesh bruised dark in his grip, juice running between his fingers. He didn't remember doing it. He touched his chest, counting his heartbeat. Thirty beats per minute. Half of what it should be. He wasn't human anymore.

"I tried to change things peacefully," Kade said, gazing at the children playing. "Thought revolution could happen without bloodshed. I was wrong."

"Would you do it differently now?" Hunter asked.

Kade was quiet for a long moment. "I don't know. Maybe. Maybe nothing. Maybe violence is the only language power understands. But I couldn't live with the blood. That's why I'm here. Hiding."

Hunter looked at the crushed apple in his hand. Dropped it. It hit the floor and split open, the flesh inside turned black where he'd touched it. Rotting from the inside out. Just like him.

"I can live with the blood, kid," Hunter said.

Kade's eyes widened. He stepped back, physically recoiled. The chevrons pulsed brighter beneath Hunter's suit.

"When you have nothing," Hunter said, his voice flat, "there's nothing to lose."

The chevrons spread up his neck. Hunter felt them moving, burrowing deeper. He didn't fight it.

For a moment, something flickered across Hunter's face. He reached out, touched Kade's shoulder. Kade flinched. Hunter's hand was ice cold, and where he touched, the chevrons beneath his suit pulsed visible through the fabric.

Hunter pulled back, staring at his hand. He'd felt nothing. Not warmth. Not skin. Not even the pressure of contact.

"I have to go," Hunter said.

"Don't let them turn you into a weapon," Kade said, his eyes desperate. "That's what Ouroboros does. They corrupt everything until it's just like them."

"Maybe I was always corrupt," Hunter said. "Maybe the Epicarp just stripped away the mask."

He walked away. Behind him, Kade stood alone, watching the children play. Hunter didn't look back.

Hunter found Arlowe waiting. She studied his face, searching.

"Did Kade help?"

Hunter said nothing. Just stared at her with those glowing eyes until she looked away.

"Hunter, the path you're on is dangerous."

"Take me to Ouroboros. Now."

She studied him for a long moment. "You've changed. Even in the last hour. I barely recognize you."

"Good."

They descended. The air grew thicker with each level. Hunter's lungs should have struggled. They didn't.

Down, down, down into sections of the Dall that felt older, darker. Alive in ways the upper levels weren't. The pristine shimmer gave way to something primal. The walls here didn't sparkle—they pulsed with a low, ominous glow. The temperature dropped. Hunter's breath should have misted in the cold. It didn't. His body temperature had adjusted, matching the environment perfectly. Another sign he wasn't human anymore.

The alien corridor narrowed. The walls seemed to press in, organic material contracting as if trying to keep them out. Or keep something else in.

Hunter's heartbeat remained steady. Thirty beats per minute. Slow and inhuman.

"Detention block seven," Arlowe said finally.

They stopped at a door bathed in purple light. "The Ouroboros inside has been here for six months. We've extracted everything we can. It's been waiting for you."

"Waiting?"

"It knew you were coming. Knew about the Epicarp. About your transformation." Arlowe's hand hovered over the door, blocking Hunter from entering. "If this goes wrong—if it takes control—"

"It won't."

"But if it does—"

"Then kill me," Hunter said. "I don't care."

Arlowe's face crumpled. For just a moment, she looked on the verge of tears.

The door liquefied. Beyond it, in the darkness, something ancient stirred. The earth shifted beneath his feet. Two eyes opened—glowing, predatory. The air tasted coppery. The scent of a thunderstorm ready to strike, like the moment before the Arcanum touched his chest and reality shattered.

And then a voice—layered, harmonic, wrong—spoke, "I've been waiting for you, fixed point."

Hunter stepped through the doorway. The chevrons flared bright, not with light, but with recognition. Like coming home.

The door sealed behind him with a wet, organic thud.

In the darkness, the Ouroboros laughed.

With perfect clarity, he couldn't tell where the Ouroboros ended and he began. The chevrons on his body synchronized with the creature's breathing, as though they shared the same heartbeat.

Maybe they always had.

part eight
trumpet heart

Hunter woke clearheaded. That was the first sign something was wrong. For weeks he had a fever of half-formed visions of Tara and Ember. Nightmares that had ripped him from sleep with sweat pouring down his temples, hands clutching his heart. Each more terrifying than dreams, more real than waking.

On this night, only a black void watched over him. The mechanical hum of the Dall regulated his sleep, his vitals, and his body temperature. He sat up in the small pod they'd given him. The alloy walls pulsed with soft bioluminescence, responding to his presence. Snakeskin scales shifted beneath his palms.

Hunter closed his eyes and tried to picture Tara's face. It took effort. He tried harder. Her eyes, were they blue or green? He'd looked into those eyes for fifteen years. Kissed her eyelids on those lazy Sunday afternoons. Watched them fill with tears when Ember was born. Blue or green? He couldn't say for certain.

Somewhere inside him, a whimper escaped. He couldn't remember the sound of her laugh. That soft snort when something genuinely surprised her. The way she'd tilt her head back, unguarded, joyful. Gone.

"Ember," he whispered. "What color is your hair?"

Panic seized him. Was it brown like his? Blonde like hers? That soft auburn that caught fire in sunlight? He had braided that hair with awful results. Brushed it before school. Pulled twigs from it after she climbed trees in the backyard. He couldn't remember how it felt between his fingers anymore, the weight, the texture, whether it was fine or thick.

Hunter pressed his palms against his eyes, searching the darkness for their faces. He found shapes, silhouettes, the ghost of a smile. But the details—the freckle on Ember's nose, the scar on Tara's chin from a childhood bike accident, melted away like snowflakes on a warm tongue.

"No," he whispered. "No, no, no."

The Dall was taking them. Not quickly, not violently, but with the patience of erosion. Each day in this place wore away another detail. Soon there'd be nothing left but names. Then not even that.

Hunter stood. Before he'd become this thing that didn't blink and whose heart beat thirty times per minute.

He left the pod and walked until he found the waterfall. It thundered in the vast space, water falling from impossible heights through the center of the Dall. Mist filtered the air, cold and clean.

Hunter stepped to the edge. Ice-cold droplets misted his face. For a moment, just a moment, he felt something real. Something sweeter. The shock of cold. The weight of water. The sting against his cheeks.

But beneath it, a low hum resonated in his chest. Not quite sound. Not quite a sensation. A frequency building, something distant approaching.

The chevrons on his hands flared. Then she was there, inside his mind, pressing against his consciousness like fingers kneading warm dough. The Arcanum. He could feel her rummaging through his thoughts, whispering things he couldn't quite hear.

"What do you want?" Hunter said aloud.

"The time is now."

The voice layered itself, his mother's voice, Tara's voice, Ember's voice, all speaking in perfect unison. "I'll show you where they are."

Hunter's chest tightened. "I'm dead, remember?"

"Are you?"

"I chose the timeline where they live. But I don't exist in it."

"I told you that you'd be the whisper where a person should have been. You exist in all timelines, fixed point."

The hum in his chest grew louder, insistent, like something calling him home.

Behind him, an alarm sounded. By the time Hunter reached the mess hall, the entire Dall had gathered. Hundreds of faces, all young, all afraid, all turning toward him as he entered.

Kade pushed through the crowd. "Hunter, what's happening?"

"The Arcanum," Hunter said. "She's calling me back."

A woman near the front gasped. "The Epicarp? You can't. You won't survive it twice."

Arlowe appeared at his side, her face pale. "Hunter, if you go back in, the transformation might be complete. You might not come out human."

"You call this human?" Hunter looked down at his hands. The chevrons were spreading again, crawling up his wrists like vines. "She told me there's another way, a way to fix it."

"That's impossible. You already chose."

"Did I?" Hunter's voice was flat. "Forcing someone's hand is the opposite of choice. If there's another way, I'm taking it."

The crowd parted as Hunter walked toward the exit. One by one, they began to follow him. Not speaking. Not touching him. Walking in a silent procession.

When they reached the Epicarp, an elderly man with kind eyes bent down and placed something at Hunter's feet. Then another person did the same. And another. Within moments, the alien corridor was lined with offerings creating a path to the dome.

Kade stood at the front, tears streaming down his face. He looked at Hunter for a long moment, then said quietly: "Don't let the blood define you."

Hunter wanted to promise he wouldn't. But he couldn't lie. Not now. Not to this kid who'd tried so hard to change the world without violence and failed. So Hunter just nodded once, then stepped onto the path.

Behind him, a sound rose from the crowd, soft clicking, hundreds of tongues against teeth. The rhythm built, overlapping, creating an ambient hum that followed him into the darkness.

The door liquefied. Hunter stepped through. Into the Epicarp. Into whatever came next.

The dome had changed. Gone were the artifacts, the crystalline structures, the sense of organized chaos. What remained was vast emptiness—a rotunda so large Hunter couldn't see its edges. The air felt thick, expectant, like the moment before lightning strikes.

Above him, the ceiling transformed. The alloy rippled and shifted, becoming transparent. Stars blazed into view. Not Earth's stars. These were older, stranger, burning with colors that had no names. The room was flying through the cosmos. Hunter's stomach lurched as constellations wheeled overhead. He was standing inside the eye beyond the dark shore, watching the birth and death of galaxies compressed into seconds.

Then the stars dimmed. A garden bloomed beneath his feet.

Emerald grass spread in all directions, soft, impossible. A stream trickled nearby, clear water flowing over smooth stones. Purple alliums swayed in a breeze that came from nowhere. The air smelled of honeysuckle and rain. And in the center of it all stood the tree.

Golden. Luminous. Bark woven with light that moved like liquid beneath the surface.

Hunter took a step closer.

Faces stared back at him from the bark. Tara's face, her expression peaceful, sleeping. Ember's face beside hers, younger, laughing at something he couldn't hear. His own face, twisted in anguish. All of them trapped in the wood grain, woven into the tree's flesh like memories made solid.

Its roots stretched across the universe, pulsing with energy. Branches reached into dimensions Hunter's eyes couldn't see, bending space itself. Hanging from the lowest branch was a single fruit.

Then he saw her. A small figure beneath the tree, playing with something in the grass.

Ember.

Not the teenager she'd become, but Ember at six years old, in her favorite yellow sundress. The one with daisies on it. She was making a chain of flowers, humming to herself.

Hunter's breath caught. His heart—that mechanical, thirty-beats-per-minute heart—stuttered.

She looked up at him and smiled. "Daddy! Come see what I made!"

He took a step toward her. Then another. She was so close. If he could just touch her, just hold her one more time—

"Beautiful, isn't it?" The Arcanum's voice, soft behind him.

Hunter turned. She stood beside the tree now, her face flickering—Tara, Ember, back to Tara. She plucked the fruit from the branch. The moment she did, the vision of Ember playing in the grass flickered like a candle flame and vanished.

"No," Hunter whispered. "Bring her back."

"Eat," the Arcanum said in Tara's voice. Soft. Gentle. Utterly wrong. She held out the fruit. It pulsed in her palm, warm and inviting, glowing with an inner light. "This will lift the veil. You'll see her again. Really see her. I promise."

Hunter stared at the fruit, hypnotized. Inside it, he could see Earth, the Dall, the Ouroboros home planet, and others he didn't recognize. All connected by golden threads that wove between worlds like a vast cosmic web.

"Tree of knowledge," the Arcanum said, and now her voice was Ember's—young, trusting. "The last doorway will close. But you'll have your revenge. You'll save them. Isn't that what you want?"

The fruit hummed in his vision, calling to him.

Hunter reached out. Took it from her hand. It was warm, almost alive, pulsing against his palm like a second heartbeat.

"This will hurt," the Arcanum whispered. Her face settled on Tara's features, and for a moment she looked sad. Almost human. "But you'll understand everything. And then you can make it right."

Hunter closed his eyes. Thought of Ember's laugh, already fading from his memory. Thought of Tara's eyes, blue or green, he still couldn't remember.

He bit down.

The flesh tasted sweet at first. Honey. Summer mornings. Tara's perfume. The taste of Ember's hair when he'd kissed the top of her head at bedtime. Every good memory he'd ever had condensed into that single bite.

He took another. Then another. The fruit was too sweet, too perfect. Juice ran down his chin, warm and golden.

Then the veil shattered.

Code flooded his mind. Not like information being fed to him—like his skull splitting open and the universe being poured directly into his brain. Coordinates. Frequencies. Quantum equations. The location of the tablet. The names of the Ouroboros leaders, their faces, their histories, their fears. The structure of the moon base, every alien corridor, every weakness. The names of fixed points across all timelines. The moment Earth falls. The moment it could be saved.

Everything too much. Far too much.

Hunter gasped. His hand was fused to it, the flesh merging with his palm, golden light spreading up his arm.

"Stop," he choked. "Please."

But the code kept coming. Faster. Deeper. Rewriting his thoughts, his memories, his very sense of self. He could feel it burrowing into his neurons, replacing synapses with circuitry, flesh with something else.

The garden flickered. The stream ran backward. The purple alliums turned black, withering.

Fire raced up his spine. Hunter screamed and fell to his knees. The chevrons erupted across his entire body—no longer just patterns beneath his skin but burning through it, fusing with bone, with nerve, with blood. He could feel them rewriting his DNA, one cell at a time.

The fruit exploded in his hands. White light erupted from the core, blinding, burning.

The garden vanished. The stars went dark. The universe itself seemed to hold its breath.

"Hunter!" Arlowe's voice, distant. "We're losing him!"

He was lying on the floor of the Epicarp. When had he fallen? The dome's walls spun around him. Or maybe he was spinning. He couldn't tell anymore.

Arlowe placed a device on his chest. "This will help with the pain."

The pain didn't stop. It intensified.

Blood poured from Hunter's nose, black, then red, then black again.

It hissed when it hit the floor, eating through the alloy like acid. His body convulsed. Every muscle locked. He couldn't breathe. Couldn't think. Could only feel the fruit's code tearing through his mind like shrapnel.

His eyes burned. Then went white. Pure, colorless white.

"Stay with us!" Arlowe shouted.

But he was already somewhere else.

He could see Tara and Ember now. Really see them. In another timeline, they were sitting at the kitchen table. Morning sunlight streamed through the window behind them, painting them in gold. Ember was doing homework, chewing on her pencil. Tara was drinking coffee, reading something on her phone.

Alive. Safe. Happy.

And they had no idea he existed.

Hunter watched Ember push her hair behind her ear—brown, he saw now, with hints of auburn in the light—and smile at something her mother said. That smile. God, that smile. He'd forgotten how it crinkled the corners of her eyes.

His heartbeat slowed. Thirty beats per minute. Twenty-five.

The chevrons spread up his neck, across his face, burning patterns into his skull. He could feel his humanity slipping away with each pulse, replaced by something colder, something designed for a single purpose.

But in that moment, watching them, he didn't care.

Hunter smiled through the blood and the pain and the dying. He reached up, touched Arlowe's cheek with trembling fingers—or maybe it was Tara's cheek, or Ember's. He couldn't tell anymore. All the timelines were collapsing into one, overlapping, bleeding together.

"I love you both," he whispered. His voice was barely audible, fractured. "I'm sorry I couldn't save you twice."

Then the euphoria hit.

Not peace. Not acceptance. Just raw, chemical euphoria flooding his brain as his body shut down. His nervous system was overloading, drowning him in endorphins to ease the transition from human to something else.

His face locked in a rictus grin. No joy, just the body's final reckoning. Euphoria masking the dying.

Hunter lay there grinning like a lunatic while Arlowe pressed devices to his chest and shouted commands he couldn't hear. Kade appeared beside her, young face twisted in horror, reaching for Hunter's hand but afraid to touch him.

The last thing Hunter saw before the darkness took him was the golden tree.

It was dying.

Branch by branch, leaf by leaf, it was turning to ash. The faces in the bark frozen mid-scream. Tara, Ember, himself, mouths open in silent anguish as the wood crumbled. The roots withered. The light dimmed.

He had eaten the last fruit. The tree of knowledge was ending.

And Hunter had killed it.

The smile stayed frozen on his face as his eyes rolled back.

Somewhere, in another timeline, Tara looked up from her coffee. Touched her chest. Frowned.

For just a moment, she felt something. Like someone watching over her. Like a presence she'd known her whole life but could never quite name. Like someone letting go.

"Mom?" Ember asked. "You okay?"

Tara blinked. The feeling passed. "Yeah, sweetie. Just... I don't know. Weird moment."

She shook her head and went back to her morning. Outside, the sun kept shining. Inside, Ember went back to her homework. Life continued, peaceful and undisturbed.

And somewhere beyond space and time, a whisper where a person should have been finally stopped screaming.

In the Epicarp, Hunter's heartbeat slowed.

Thirty beats per minute.

The chevrons pulsed once, brilliant gold, lighting the entire dome.

Twenty beats.

The patterns began to fade, sinking deeper into his flesh until they disappeared beneath the surface entirely. His skin looked almost normal now. Almost human.

Ten beats.

The garden was gone. The tree was ash. Nothing remained but Hunter's body on the cold floor.

Five.

Arlowe pressed her fingers to his neck, searching for a pulse.

"Is he?" the apprentice whispered behind her.

"I don't know."

Around them, the dome began to crack. Spiderweb fissures spread across the ceiling where the tree's roots had been, growing wider with each passing second. The Epicarp was dying too. Whatever Hunter had done, whatever he'd become, had broken something fundamental in the fabric of this place.

One beat.

Then silence.

Arlowe closed her eyes. Kade turned away, shoulders shaking.

The age of knowledge was ending.

And somewhere on Earth, deep in the chest of every living human, a sound began. Not heard with ears but felt in the marrow. A vibration that rattles teeth and bone.

The second trumpet, echoing inside his heart.

Ouroboros smiled in the darkness and whispered: *HE'S READY.*

The age of war—inevitable.

part nine
the unmaking

The droids went haywire the moment Hunter's feet touched the floor. Radiant spheres that had been dormant suddenly rose, circling him frantically. Their lights flickered purple instead of white.

"Three days." Arlowe's fingers flew across the display panel, her jaw tight. "You've been out three days, and now you're crashing my medical bay." The screen went dark under her touch. "They've locked me out."

He wasn't controlling them. Not consciously. But the fruit—the code it had poisoned him with was giving commands through his body. The medical bed tilted ninety degrees behind him with a pneumatic hiss, forcing him upright. His spine ached with a pain that felt distant, as if it belonged to someone else.

"The fruit?" His voice came out hoarse, tasting of copper.

She stepped closer, studying the chevrons that had stopped spreading. They covered him completely now, frozen in their final pattern like circuitry etched in glass. Her hand hovered near his shoulder, then withdrew. "It gave you what you needed." A pause. "How much of you is still in there?"

Hunter closed his eyes. Coordinates flooded his mind. Frequencies. Names—some he didn't recognize yet. And one name he did, Madam Synod. The location of the device. The structure of the Ouroboros moon base. Every secret the fruit had contained. And beneath it all, a voice, not the Arcanum's. Guiding him. Pulling him toward something.

"The Time Recorder." He opened his eyes. "I need to see it."

Arlowe's expression darkened. "You're not ready."

"I don't care." The room tilted, then steadied. The nanites in the walls hummed, responding to his presence. "It has information I need. The fruit is only part of it."

She held his gaze for a long moment. Whatever she saw there made her step back. "They almost have you completely. When they do—"

"I won't exist if I don't try."

Arlowe reached for a panel and retrieved the neural-adaptive suit. "Put this on." She tossed it to him. "Then we go."

Hunter's hand shook as he reached for the suit. The fabric recoiled from his touch, sensing the chevrons, recognizing him as other. He forced it on anyway. The suit screamed against his skin, a high-pitched whine only he could hear.

Thousands of nanites swarmed his body before he could seal the seams. Not attacking, responding to invisible commands. They covered him in seconds, a diamond cocoon that pulsed with purple light. The nanites felt like static electricity crawling across every nerve ending.

Arlowe dove behind the medical console. "Hunter—"

He could feel the nanites interfacing with the chevrons, syncing with the code the fruit had given him. His body temperature spiked, then plummeted. His vision shifted, and suddenly he could see heat signatures bleeding through the walls, electromagnetic fields pulsing like veins through the Dall's infrastructure. The air tasted like ozone and something older, decay that transcended biology.

Purple lightning arced from his shoulders. His feet left the ground.

For a moment, he hung suspended in the air. Then he opened his mouth and screamed. Not in pain, but in code. Static frequencies that shouldn't have existed in human vocal cords. The sound harmonized with the chamber's groaning metal.

"I see it!" The words fractured into dozens of voices speaking through him. His body convulsed, spine arching. "The tablet, I see where it is!"

The sonic wave erupted from him. The ceiling shattered. Cracks spider-webbed across the alloy, and for a brief second, Arlowe could see through to the level above, figures frozen mid-stride, faces turned toward the sound. Then everything went dark.

The nanites scattered, retreating into the walls like roaches from light. Hunter collapsed.

"Lights!" Arlowe shouted.

The system flickered angrily, strobing. In the rapid bursts, she saw him curled on the ground, purple vapor rising from his skin. She fought through the time distortion, each step feeling like wading through mud, air pressing against her eardrums like deep water, and reached him.

"Can you hear me?" She grabbed his face, her grip the only solid thing in a tilting world. "Hunter!"

His eyes were white. "The code." He gasped, tasting metal, his own blood from biting his cheek. "It's not over. It's here." He tapped his skull.

She pulled him upright, his weight sagging against her. "Stay with me."

"The Time Recorder." His pupils flickered back for a moment, black against the white. "The voice won't stop. It knows where the tablet is. I need the Time Recorder."

"If you go in there like this, it'll kill you before we get the information." She held his gaze. "What if it's a trick to get the code?"

Hunter smiled, broken glass across his face. "I'm betting on it."

This isn't me.

THIS ISN'T?

But it was. The code didn't make him cruel. It just removed the leash.

They descended through levels of the Dall that grew darker with each step. Word had spread. The fixed point was going to face the Time Recorder. By the time they reached the detention wing, hundreds lined the grand hall in silence. An old woman pressed her palm to the floor where Hunter had walked. A child tried to collect the purple vapor in cupped hands. Someone was praying in a language that predated the Dall itself.

As Hunter passed, they began placing purple alliums on the floor.

He moved forward, feet barely touching the ground. The code guided him, pulling him toward his target.

At the threshold stood two Keepers, older than anyone Hunter had seen in the Dall. Their faces were weathered by centuries of guarding this place. Their eyes tracked him with ancient precision.

"Stand back." One raised a hand, voice like gravel. "You have no authority here."

The door liquefied before he could finish, metal flowing like mercury, pooling at the threshold.

"Keepers." A woman approached with a stride that commanded space, her voice silk over steel. "Let him pass."

The Keepers immediately saluted. "Yes, Madam Synod."

"Ma'am." Arlowe's salute was crisp, military.

Madam Synod's gaze settled on Hunter, calculating, measuring. "The Arcanum has informed me you would need guidance." She gestured to the door. "The Time Recorder has been waiting for you. All eyes are upon you now."

Even through the fog of transformation, he recognized power when he saw it. She had seen this before. He could see it in the way she stood, too still, like someone bracing for impact.

He nodded and stepped through the doorway. It sealed behind him with a wet, organic thud.

The chamber was dark and vast. The stench hit him, sour and stagnant, like a lizard tank left to rot. Slime-coated walls absorbed light rather than reflecting it, creating a void that pressed against his eyes. Silence pressed against his eardrums. But the code gave him sight even here, thermal, electromagnetic, dimensional.

There, in the corner, a glow flickered like dying embers.

"I see you." Hunter moved closer, fists clenched. "You cannot hide from me."

The Time Recorder scuttled from the shadows. It was Ouroboros, but corrupted. Scales cracked like old porcelain. Body hunched from centuries in captivity. When it opened its eyes, the glow flickered yellow. Its tongue lashed out, sampling the air between them.

BECAUSE YOU ARE ONE OF US. The hiss echoed off wet walls.

Hunter could sense the crowd watching through some mechanism he didn't understand. The Dall was broadcasting this confrontation. Hundreds of eyes, waiting.

"Then you know why I'm here."

The Time Recorder laughed, wet, gurgling sounds that bounced off the slick walls. "Can you feel it? You already know the answer."

"Where is it?" Hunter's voice sliced through the void.

I CAN SMELL ITS SWEETNESS ON YOU. The creature's tongue lashed out again, sampling Hunter's essence. *TELL ME, WAS IT EVERYTHING YOU HOPED FOR?*

Without conscious thought, Hunter reached out with his mind. Invisible force seized the Time Recorder by the throat and lifted it off the ground. The creature thrashed, clawing at its neck, eyes bulging. Its scales scraped together, a sound like knives on ceramic.

"You enjoy terrorizing these people." Hunter's eyes glowed white. "They would applaud if I ended you right now."

"We need the Time Recorder alive." Madam Synod's voice entered the void somehow. "For now."

The creature's struggles intensified. Then Hunter felt it, a signal trying to escape through their mental connection. The Time Recorder was using him as a conduit, trying to send a message to the moon.

"It is using me." Hunter's voice carried to those watching. "Trying to contact Ouroboros headquarters."

"Did the transmission go through?" Madam Synod's voice remained measured, formal.

"No." Hunter smiled coldly. "Should I continue?"

She paused, then said, "I am curious to see where this goes."

The Time Recorder stopped struggling and opened its mind. Centuries of memories flooded through. Thousands of human deaths, cities burning, children screaming. The Time Recorder had recorded it all, cataloging humanity's suffering for the Ouroboros archives. Feasting on fear like something exquisite and forbidden.

Hunter saw himself in those memories. Multiple versions across multiple timelines. Always failing. Always alone. Always ending up dead on a sidewalk somewhere, tumbling through the universe as a fixed point for eternity.

I SEE YOUR DEATH. The Time Recorder's telepathic whisper

slithered through his mind like snake oil. *NO MATTER HOW HARD YOU TRY, YOU TUMBLE THROUGH THE UNIVERSE AS A FIXED POINT FOR ETERNITY, SPRAWLED OUT LIKE TRASH.*

Hunter released his grip slightly. The creature smiled with its mangled face. Then Hunter saw it, something the creature was trying to hide, buried beneath layers of memory. The tablet's location, pulsing like a beacon.

"You have overstayed your welcome." Hunter's grip tightened.

WHO NEEDS THE TABLET MORE. The creature's tongue lashed desperately. *THEM OR YOU?*

Hunter reached deeper. Not for information, but for the creature's essence. Its existence across timelines. "You are not superior. Your kind just got a head start." He paused. "And that ends now."

"Hunter, that is enough!" Madam Synod's voice carried a lethal warning.

He wasn't listening. The Time Recorder had shown him Tara and Ember dying. Had cataloged their deaths, recorded their fear, feasted on it. Had laughed about it afterward.

Tara would have stopped me. Ember would have.

They weren't here. And that was the Time Recorder's fault.

Something inside Hunter broke. Maybe it had been broken all along, and the code had simply revealed it.

The creature's eyes didn't disintegrate. Hunter was more precise than that. He unmade them. One moment they existed. The next, they didn't. Not destroyed, erased, as if they had never been there at all.

The Time Recorder's scream shattered what remained of Hunter's humanity.

He peeled scales. One at a time, exposing black hollows beneath, not flesh, not blood, absence. Each scale was a window to another dimension.

That's what he told himself. The truth was simpler, he wanted it to hurt.

Thread by thread. Timeline by timeline. Hunter watched the Time Recorder's existence unravel. In one reality, the creature was young, scales pristine. In another, it had just consumed its first human fear. In a third, it was recording Ember's final breath.

He erased them all.

The creature didn't understand what was happening until it was already gone.

Black voids appeared where scales had been. The Time Recorder thrashed and howled. Its consciousness battered against Hunter's mind, showing him visions meant to break him. Tara's face at the moment of impact, Ember's last breath, his own death played across a thousand timelines.

HAVE YOU NOT FIGURED IT OUT YET? The creature gasped, its voice fracturing. *YOU HUMANS ARE ONE-DIMENSIONAL. WE LOVE YOUR IGNORANCE. YOU NEED THE PRISON WE HAVE CREATED.*

Hunter peeled another scale. The void gaped wider: *YOUR HEART IS BLACKER THAN OURS.*

"Perhaps." He ripped away another. The Time Recorder collapsed, its body riddled with absence.

PLEASE. The creature whimpered, voice like steam escaping a valve. *NO MORE.*

"That is enough!" Madam Synod shouted from beyond the chamber.

Hunter leaned closer. "Tell her you can take it."

The creature screamed like a tea kettle boiling over.

Purple smoke poured from Hunter's mouth. Nanites that had been dormant inside him, absorbed during the medical chamber incident. They looked like the ghosts of pain never spoken.

He knelt before the Time Recorder and met its eyeless gaze. "The war starts with you."

The creature smiled with its demolished face, black hollows weeping absence: *WE HAVE DONE THIS BEFORE. OUR PATHS ALWAYS INTERSECT. YOU ARE ONE OF US.*

"Wrong." Hunter's eyes beamed with white light. "I am the improved model."

Then he unmade it.

Not with violence, with absence. Hunter reached into every timeline where the Time Recorder existed and erased it. One by one, thread by thread, he severed the creature's connection to reality. The chamber filled with the sound of reality tearing, wet fabric ripping in slow motion.

It laughed as it died. Screamed. Laughed again. Until the void silenced it completely.

The moment the Time Recorder ceased to exist, Hunter's power detonated.

Time itself fractured. Everyone outside the chamber froze mid-motion, then fast-forwarded, then froze again. Reality stuttered, trying to compensate for the temporal wound he had torn open. The walls groaned, metal shrieking.

Hunter's voice fragmented across multiple timelines. "I cannot stop it!"

But no one could reach him. The energy bubble he had created was impenetrable. The crowd outside toppled backward as the shockwave expanded, bodies moving in slow motion, then fast, then not at all.

He watched it all happen. Trapped in the space between moments, unable to move, his body threatening to merge with the alloy as reality tried to find somewhere to put him. His fingertips were translucent, as if he had begun erasing himself in the process.

The chamber exploded.

The universe went white.

When the light faded, Hunter lay motionless on the chamber floor. Blood leaked from his nose, his ears, the corners of his eyes. Not red, purple, laced with code.

The Time Recorder was gone. Erased so completely that the Dall's systems couldn't register it had ever existed.

Arlowe was the first to reach him. She pressed her fingers against his neck, her hand shaking. "Thirty beats per minute." Her voice cracked. "He's barely holding on."

"He killed it." Someone in the crowd whispered, the words carrying through the silence.

"He erased it." Another corrected, voice hushed with something like reverence. Or fear.

Madam Synod stood at the threshold, dust-streaked, her usual composure cracked. Her hand trembled against the doorframe as she watched Hunter's chest rise and fall. "The fixed has risen." Her whisper carried through the silence like a prayer. Or a curse.

She had seen this before.

Kade pushed through the crowd, tears streaming. "Is he—" His voice broke. "Tell me he's breathing."

"Alive." Arlowe's fingers pressed harder against his neck, feeling each sluggish beat. "Barely."

"Did he get the information?" Kade's knees hit the floor beside him.

Arlowe stared at the space where the Time Recorder had been, at the scorch marks spreading across the floor like bacteria. "He got everything." She paused, checking her weapon's charge. "And they will know it the second he wakes up."

"Then they will come for him." Kade's voice was hollow.

"Let them." Arlowe's hand went to her weapon. "I have been waiting."

The chevrons pulsed once beneath Hunter's skin, responding to her touch.

In the silence that followed, the purple alliums the crowd had laid began to glow. Softly at first, then brighter, until the entire galactic corridor was lit by their bioluminescence. Hunter had changed them too. Even unconscious, he was rewriting reality.

Around them, the Dall's walls groaned. Cracks spread through the alloy. Whatever Hunter had done in that chamber had damaged something fundamental, not just the structure, but the fabric of time itself.

The age of hiding was over.

And Hunter Persefoni, whatever he had become, was their weapon.

In the rubble, something stirred. A single scale from the Time Recorder, still intact. Still recording.

It pulsed once with yellow light, then went dark.

part ten
john 3:33

Hunter choked on his own vomit. Stomach acid curdled and burned his throat. Metallic taste flooded his mouth, something more alien than copper, than blood. He rolled onto his side, retching, and watched black liquid spill onto concrete. Black. He blinked. The puddle was red now. Normal blood. His blood. He blinked again. Black.

The chevrons pulsed once, hot beneath his skin, then faded. Hunter stared at his palm. Smooth. No markings. He turned his hand over. There, scales forming like living tattoos, then dissolving, like watching time-lapse footage of a wound healing and reopening simultaneously.

A voice boomed from somewhere: "Yo, golden boy finally woke up! Daddy's lawyers coming for you?"

His head lolled to the side. Cinder blocks. Metal door. Halogen light buzzing like insects trapped in amber. Jail. The Dall was gone. The Time Recorder was gone. And he had no idea how he'd gotten here.

He pushed himself upright, head throbbing. The air was thick with the stench of piss, shit, and something floral, lavender, maybe, trying desperately to mask the rot beneath. His clothes stuck to his skin, drenched in sweat.

Thunder rolled through his skull, absent of sound, only sensation. The cell flickered. For a split second, the walls were glass, crystalline like the Dall. Then back to the cinder block. The toilet flickered. Porcelain. Steel. Porcelain. His pulse hammered, nearly a single continuous flutter.

"I'm in multiple timelines at once." Hunter's voice came out hoarse.

More voices erupted in the distance. Laughter, howls, the sound of fists pounding metal.

Someone screamed, "Southie! Southie! Southie!" The word traveled from cell to cell like an infection. Each inmate took up the chant until the entire pod shook with it. An alarm blared. The floor vibrated beneath his body, and suddenly everything went silent.

"Pipe down in there!" A gruff voice cut through the quiet. "I'll lock the whole thing down like last time."

"Hey, Sarge! It's not our fault. Dude over here woke up. He woke up!"

"Hands on the wall. Don't make me put you in solitary."

Footsteps approached, then a face appeared in the door's slot—a middle-aged man, square jaw, eyes that seemed days from retirement. "Son of a bitch is alive."

"Where am I?" Hunter said.

"Detectives have been camping outside your cell for two days." The sergeant smiled, but those flat eyes didn't. "Never seen Williams this patient."

The door buzzed, unlocked. The sergeant entered with a younger deputy trailing behind. "Up on those feet, boy. We're gonna get you cleaned up."

The deputy pulled Hunter from the floor. "Ooh, damn! This one hasn't rotated in a while."

"No shit. Get him hosed down and take him down for questioning."

The shower water hit Hunter's skin, scalding hot. He gasped, jumped back. The water was ice cold now. Had it been the whole time? He pressed his palm to the tile wall. Smooth concrete. He blinked. Rough brick. Concrete again.

The timelines are bleeding together.

When he looked down, his hand was bleeding. Not bleeding—weeping. Black liquid seeped from beneath his fingernails, thick as oil. He watched it swirl down the drain. Red now. His blood, normal human blood. He blinked. Black again, and something was moving in it, tiny geometric patterns like circuit boards dissolving in water.

He scrubbed his palm against the tile until skin tore. Pain lanced up his arm, sharp and anchoring. The physical sensation grounded him momentarily. Red blood. Only red. He breathed. Counted to ten. Looked again.

Black drops spiraled down the drain, forming chevron patterns in the water.

The smell hit him, ozone, like lightning had struck inside the building. Then it was gone, replaced by the stench of mildew and cheap soap.

The tiles flickered. White. Black. Cracked. Whole. White again.

"You done in there?" The deputy's voice rang through his skull.

Hunter blinked. The blood was gone. He dried off and dressed in the same clothes he'd put on before heading to the manor, the night he killed the blonde masquerading as human.

They led him down corridors that stretched too long, then compressed like accordions. Other inmates watched from cells, faces flickering between human and something else, reptilian features phasing in and out of focus. Hunter kept his eyes down. Counted his steps. Thirty-seven. Or three hundred seventy. The numbers wouldn't hold still.

They reached an interrogation room. Tattered chairs. Camera in the corner. Two-way mirror reflecting Hunter's haggard face back at him. But no red light on the camera. No handcuffs. The door had a window, unlocked.

This doesn't make sense.

He sat there for some time, trying to piece together what happened. The last thing he remembered was the Dall. Killing the Time Recorder. The explosion of power. Then nothing. Just darkness and waking up here.

Sharp prickles electrified the back of his neck. The room swayed. He gripped the edge of the table, pulse pounding in his throat. Not now. Stay conscious.

The lights went out.

"Did you have a good nap?" A man's voice, smooth, commanding.

His vision swam, unfocused and hazy. He raised his head and saw the outline of someone sitting across from him.

"We have a saying around here," the lieutenant continued. "Criminals sleep soundly after they get caught."

"Why am I here?" Hunter's voice cracked.

A different voice from behind said, "You don't remember?"

"I can't see." Hunter blinked hard, and slowly the man's face came into focus.

The lieutenant's deep brown skin caught the light, his jaw chiseled like stone, and his eyes shifting between blue and gray like a storm about to break. Hunter had seen those eyes before. Somewhere. Sometime. Another timeline. The room flickered briefly, became a Dall pod with crystalline walls, then snapped back to cinder block and mirrors.

"Your eyes look fine to me, Mr. Persefoni." The lieutenant leaned back. "What exactly do you remember?"

"I don't know."

"You don't know, or you don't remember?" The lieutenant gave him a searching look. "Is something wrong with your ears too, Mr. Persefoni?"

Hunter said nothing.

"I guess it's the hard way." The lieutenant's tone hardened. "Take Mr. Persefoni back to his cell. Let him cool down for a while."

"I want my attorney," Hunter said quickly.

The man behind him, the detective, snarled, "You think money buys you out of double homicide? I'm gonna make sure you rot."

"Hold on, Detective." The lieutenant raised a hand. "You have to forgive my partner. He's been under a lot of stress after two officers died in the line of duty a few nights ago."

Pain throbbed through Hunter's hand. He looked down. The chevrons were there—faint purple lines crawling up his wrist like veins. Then gone.

"Are you?" the lieutenant said.

"Am I what?"

"Ready to tell the truth?"

"Yes!" Hunter's voice rose. Then everything went quiet.

"Mr. Persefoni?"

"Person of interest," Hunter muttered. Whatever else the lieutenant said came in static and fragments.

"You are being questioned at the Southampton Police Department," Williams said, voice calm and coordinated. "My partner and I recovered you from Flying Point Road."

"Do you own a vintage white Porsche convertible, Mr. Persefoni?" Spencer spat, stretching the name like something that didn't belong in his mouth.

Flying Point Road hit Hunter like a punch to the gut. Barbara's severed head. Mayer's body slumped in the chair. The word escaped before he could stop it. "Shit."

Williams' eyes sparked with satisfaction.

"My memory's... fragmented." Hunter stumbled over the words.

"What were you doing out there at three in the morning?" Williams raised an eyebrow.

"That night is blank." Everything around him blurred and warped.

"The blonde woman. Names." Williams' voice cut sharp as a scalpel.

Hunter froze. Copper taste flooded his mouth. Williams' face flickered, younger, no scars. Older, half his face burned. Back to normal.

"Mr. Persefoni?" Williams leaned forward.

Pain throbbed through his hand again. He clenched his fist, hiding the chevrons that pulsed beneath his skin.

"I can't separate what happened from what I thought happened." He seemed on the verge of throwing up. "I need my attorney."

Spencer kicked the back of Hunter's chair. "You're not going anywhere until we get some answers!"

"Detective!" Williams snapped. "That's enough!"

Hunter's nose erupted, blood streaming down his face. Black drops hit the table. Williams stared. The drops turned red.

Hunter wiped his nose with the back of his hand. The blood was gone. Had it ever been there? Or was his mind bleeding between timelines, showing him things that existed only in other realities?

"Mr. Persefoni, if you're being coerced in any way, we can protect you."

Hunter saw it, the execution replaying in Williams' mind, the Smith sisters standing over bodies, shadow figures reaching down, pulling them back from death. The images weren't memory. They were happening now, in real time, bleeding through from Williams' thoughts into Hunter's fragmenting consciousness.

Thunder rolled through Hunter's skull. Williams' face flickered. Dead. Alive. Dead. Alive.

"The shadow figures," Hunter said, as though it finally clicked in his brain.

"Shadow figures?" Williams said.

Footsteps in the hallway. Multiple people. Williams' jaw tightened.

Three people in expensive suits entered the room.

"Thank God," Hunter said.

A man stepped forward, Hunter's attorney. "Gentlemen. My client's medical condition requires immediate release. I trust we won't need to involve the DA's office again." He slapped papers on the table, placed a pen in front of Hunter. "Sign this, Mr. Persefoni. This is a property release."

Williams hit the table. "You must have a lot of money, Mr. Persefoni."

The shorter attorney stepped forward. "We intend on filing a civil suit against this police department for unlawful detainment."

Williams stood slowly. He walked to a cabinet and pulled out a clear plastic bag. Inside: dark clothes, a wallet, and a Rolex. He slid the bag across the table. "These are your personal effects. Sign here."

Hunter stared at the bag. The watch face stared back. His throat closed. That watch. The one Tara had clasped around his wrist on their fifth anniversary, her fingers warm, her smile bright. So you'll always know when to come home, she'd said. He'd been wearing it when she died. When everything changed.

His hand shot across the table before he could stop himself, fingers clawing at the plastic.

"Where did you get this?" The words came out strangled, broken.

"Crash scene on Flying Point. Vintage Porsche wrapped around a tree. You were there, remember?" Williams studied him with predator's eyes. "That watch mean something to you?"

Hunter picked up the bag with shaking hands. The watch face was visible through the plastic. The hands were frozen at 3:33. The exact moment the transformation began. When Tara died. When the timeline split. When everything restarted, all at once.

The bag slipped from his trembling fingers, hit the table with a dull thud.

Hunter's chevrons exploded across his hand. Not tattoos. Not scars. Living marks, geometric and alien, crawling up from his wrist like vines seeking sunlight. They pulsed faintly purple, then brighter, casting shadows that didn't match the room's lighting.

Williams jerked back. His chair screamed across linoleum. Spencer's hand flew to his holster. The attorneys froze mid-motion, briefcases suspended in air like time had stopped.

The burnt copper smell flooded the room. Williams gagged. Spencer covered his nose with his sleeve. The attorneys exchanged glances—they smelled it too. Proof that what they were seeing was real.

"What the fuck is that?!" Williams' voice cracked. Hunter heard genuine fear in it—not cop fear, not tactical fear. Primal fear.

Hunter looked up. His eyes flickered, not quite human anymore. Shifting between colors, between timelines.

"Three thirty-three," Hunter whispered. "Jeremiah 33:3. 'Call to me, and I will answer you, and show you great and mighty things.'"

The words felt foreign in his mouth. Not John. Jeremiah. But why couldn't he remember? The timelines were scrambling even his memories of scripture.

The chevrons faded. His eyes returned to normal. Williams stepped back, hand on his weapon, thumb releasing the holster strap. "Who the hell are you?"

Hunter stood, clutching the bag. The watch pulsed in his hand—he could feel it through the plastic, beating in rhythm with his heartbeat. "Someone who's been calling for help." Hunter met Williams' eyes one last time. "And something answered."

His attorney grabbed Hunter's arm. "We're leaving. Now."

Williams watched them go, frozen in place. As Hunter reached the door, he looked back.

For a split second, Williams saw them, the chevrons crawling up Hunter's neck, across his face, covering him like scales. Then they were gone.

Just a man in dark clothes, walking away.

But Williams knew better. He knew Jeremiah 33:3. Every cop who'd worked too many nightshift murders knew it. The verse about calling into darkness and getting answers you didn't want.

He'd seen the truth.

And there was no going back.

Outside, the precinct parking lot stretched before him. His attorney was still talking, something about civil suits, about keeping quiet, about damage control. But Hunter wasn't listening. He held the plastic bag against his chest, feeling the watch pulse in rhythm with his heartbeat.

The watch whispered: Three-thirty-three.

The moment he'd called for help. The moment something answered. The moment Tara died and he became... this.

He looked back through the precinct glass. Williams stood in the interrogation room, frozen, staring at his own shaking hands.

He saw the truth, Hunter thought. And now we're both damned.

The attorney opened the car door. Hunter slid inside, still clutching the bag. Through the tinted window, he watched Williams finally move, collapsing into a chair, head in his hands.

Two men who'd called into darkness.

Two men who'd received answers.

And neither would ever be the same.

part eleven
the release

Hunter followed Tom through the police station, attorneys flanking him like bodyguards. His hand wouldn't stop shaking. The watch pulsed in his pocket, he could feel it through the plastic bag, warm against his thigh.

The watch ticked. Three-thirty-three.

Officers stared as they passed. Some with curiosity. Others with something darker, recognition, maybe. As if they could see what Williams had seen. The chevrons lurking beneath his skin.

"Keep walking," Tom muttered. "Don't look at anyone. Don't say anything."

They pushed through the front doors into blinding sunlight. Hunter stumbled, raising his hand to shield his eyes. The world tilted. Copper taste flooded his mouth. For a split second, the parking lot was empty. Then filled with cars. Empty again.

The seven-hour cycle. It's speeding up.

"Mr. Persefoni?" Tom gripped his elbow. "You with me?"

Hunter blinked. The parking lot stabilized. Three identical black sedans idled at the curb, engines purring.

"Which one?" Hunter said.

Tom pointed to the middle car. "That one. The driver will take you somewhere safe."

"You're not coming?"

"My job was to get you out." Tom pressed a business card into Hunter's hand. "You need something else, you call that number. Day or night."

Hunter looked at the card. The letters swam, rearranged themselves. He blinked hard. Normal again.

"Go," Tom said. "Before they change their minds."

Tom watched from the station steps as Hunter climbed into the sedan. Then he turned and walked back inside, already pulling out his phone.

Hunter slid into the back seat. The privacy window was already up, tinted so dark he couldn't see the driver. The leather was cold beneath him despite the sun beating down. The door locks clicked. The car pulled away from the curb, smooth and silent.

Hunter watched the police station shrink in the side mirror. Williams stood on the front steps, watching. Even from this distance, Hunter could see the lieutenant's hand resting on his weapon.

He's afraid of me now.

The thought should have satisfied him. Instead, it made his chest tighten.

"Where are we going?" Hunter said to the privacy window.

No answer.

He knocked on the glass. "Hello?"

Nothing.

Thunder rolled through his skull again. The car's interior flickered. For a moment, the seats were white instead of black. The dashboard was different. Then back to normal. Hunter pressed his palm against the window. His reflection stared back, eyes shifting between colors. Green. Brown. Something else. Purple, maybe.

He looked away.

The car turned onto a service road, then into the back lot of Montauk Plaza train station. Two more identical sedans were already there, noses facing a wooded area. The driver pulled in between them, killing the engine.

The privacy window lowered.

Evelyne sat in the driver's seat, turned to face him. But something was off. Her hair was longer. A scar above her left eyebrow that hadn't been there before—or had it? Hunter couldn't remember anymore. The timelines were bleeding together, bringing versions of people he knew but didn't quite know.

Her eyes were red, like she'd been crying. But her expression was steel.

"We don't have much time," she said.

"Evelyne." Hunter blinked. "What the hell is going on?"

"Give me your clothes."

"What?"

"Everything you're wearing is being tracked." She reached back and handed him a duffel bag. "Put this on instead."

Hunter unzipped the bag. Inside: dark pants, a shirt, and something else. Something glowing. An orb covered in crystalline spikes, pulsing with white light.

"What is this?" Hunter's hand hovered over it.

"Take off your clothes," Evelyne said. "Grab the orb. It'll do the rest."

"Evelyne—"

"They're closing in on us fast." Her voice cracked slightly. "Ouroboros. If they catch you, all of this was for nothing."

Hunter shed his clothes quickly, tossing them to the floor. He reached into the bag, hesitating. The orb looked deadly, like a weapon from another world.

"It's not doing anything," Hunter said.

Evelyne grabbed his wrist and shoved his hand into the bag. "Just like that."

The moment Hunter's fingers touched the orb, it exploded with light. Not heat, cold. A liquid cold that spread from his hand up his arm, across his chest, down to his feet. The orb went black. Then burst again, this time coating him in something viscous and alive. It crawled across his skin like living mercury, vibrating, tingling.

The Dall's alloy. He recognized it now. The same material that had covered him when he destroyed the Time Recorder.

"Now what?" Hunter said, watching the alloy settle into a second skin.

"Leave the bag. The driver will handle it." Evelyne pointed to the car on the right. "Get in that one."

Hunter stared at her. "You can't be serious."

"Do it now." Her eyes flashed. "Don't hesitate. Because if you do, they'll kill me, and they'll kill you too."

Hunter got out, skin still tingling from the alloy. He glanced back at Evelyne through the window. She was crying now, tears streaming down her face as she placed something on the seat, a thin piece of glass that glowed faintly.

She mouthed something. I'm sorry.

Then she was gone, replaced by the driver from before, a man Hunter didn't recognize.

Hunter ran to the other sedan and threw himself into the back seat. Evelyne was already there, but how? He'd just seen her in the other car. Unless...

"Three cars. Three different points in time," she said, reading his confusion. "We entered each one simultaneously from three different timelines. By the time the Ouroboros trace the tracking devices in your clothes, they'll chase the decoy car while we slip through." She smiled grimly. "The shell game only works if the shells exist in different moments."

Hunter's head spun. "That's—"

"Impossible?" Evelyne's smile faded. "You're covered in living metal that exists outside of time. Impossible stopped meaning anything the moment you became a fixed point."

A woman in her early twenties stepped out from the shadows near the car Evelyne had been driving, pilot's cap cinched tight like a badge of rank. Her deep bronze skin and hair cut clean against the cream fabric of her blouse, sharp enough to catch the eye and hold it. White pinstripes sliced down her slacks, neat as flight paths—too neat for this place. But it was the eyes that nailed Hunter from where he sat. Green and unnatural. They burned low and steady, like a fire that had been waiting for him.

Hunter couldn't look away. The woman knocked on the window.

Evelyne ignored her, staring straight ahead. The woman knocked louder. Harder.

"I think your apprentice has something urgent to tell you," Hunter said.

"She's not my apprentice." Evelyne's jaw tightened. "She doesn't follow directions very well. Reminds me of someone."

The woman banged on the glass, determined.

"She looks determined," Hunter said.

Evelyne rolled down the window halfway. "What is it?"

The woman peered through, locking eyes on Hunter immediately. "I just wanted to make sure you guys are okay before I take off."

Hunter gave a friendly wave. "We appreciate your concern, but we must be heading off before Ouroboros kills us all."

"Hunter," Evelyne warned.

But Hunter couldn't stop staring at the woman's eyes. They summoned something from deep inside him, a memory locked behind a door, bolted down, key thrown away.

I know those eyes.

"Be careful," the woman said, voice overprotective. Like she cared too much. Like he mattered to her in a way he couldn't understand.

Hunter leaned forward. "I know you, don't I? Your eyes—"

Something flickered in her expression. Hope, maybe. Desperate, fragile hope.

"Do you?" Her voice came out barely a whisper. "Do you know me?"

Hunter searched his fractured memories. Timelines overlapped, faces blurred. "I... I can't..."

Her face crumpled. Not quite crying, but close. Her hand reached toward the window, fingers splaying against the glass like she wanted to touch him but couldn't cross the barrier between them. She looked at him like he'd just torn out her heart and handed it back.

"It's okay," she whispered, more to herself than him. "You will. Someday."

Then she pulled away, and Hunter felt something inside him break. A connection severed before he even understood it existed.

"Once we get the device, we'll all be free," Evelyne said, voice tight.

"You can't see it now, but I've seen it. I promise things will work out. Now get that car out of here. Do not stop for anyone or anything, do you understand? Do it exactly how we practiced."

The woman pulled back. "I won't stop. I promise. I'll get it there safely."

"Okay, that's enough." Evelyne closed the window. She leaned back, exhaling hard.

"That whole thing was weird, don't you think?" Hunter said, watching the woman sprint to the other car. "Who is she?"

"It's you." Evelyne's voice was soft. "She wanted to see you."

"I think I know her. Those eyes."

"Drop it, okay? It won't matter after—"

"After what?" Hunter's voice rose. "Everyone keeps saying that. After I get the tablet. After we're free. What does this tablet even do? Everyone keeps talking about it like it's the answer to everything, but no one will tell me what it is!"

Evelyne's jaw tightened. "It's a Synod device. A key. It can lock or unlock fixed points—stabilize you or erase you completely. The Ouroboros want it to control the timelines. We need it to survive them." She met his eyes. "Without it, the chevrons will keep spreading until there's nothing left of who you were. The tablet is the only thing that can stop your transformation before it consumes you."

Hunter looked at his hand. The chevrons pulsed beneath his skin. "And if I don't find it?"

"Then you become what they are. Ouroboros. A creature outside time, feeding on fixed points to sustain yourself. You'll forget Tara. Forget Ember. Forget everyone you ever loved." Her voice cracked. "I've seen it happen to others. I won't let it happen to you."

The woman's car peeled out of the lot, tires squealing. Hunter watched it disappear. That green-eyed stranger who looked at him like he was her whole world.

"Are you leaving me here all alone?" Hunter said.

"I can't stay with you." Evelyne pulled out another piece of glass, handed it to the driver. "I have a meeting." She opened the door, hesitated, then looked back at him. "I want you to know that I did this for us."

"I know."

But something in her expression said that wasn't true. That there was more. Something she couldn't tell him.

"Hugo will help you," Evelyne said. "Just like he helped me."

"You go, go. He will be good, good." A voice from the front seat.

Hunter jumped. Two men materialized in the driver and passenger seats. Thin vapor coalescing into solid forms. Shadow figures. The same men from the airport.

One had a purple gash on his neck, deep as a canyon. The other's clothes were ripped, revealing more of that alloy material beneath.

"Are we too late?" Evelyne asked.

The shadow figure's voice strained. "There's still time, but we need to hurry. The Rippling is unfolding faster than before. Timelines collapsing into each other like dominoes. We can't keep the portal open for much longer."

"The Rippling?" Hunter said.

Evelyne turned to him, face grave. "The end of linear time. When all timelines exist simultaneously, reality fractures. Everything that was, is, and will happen at once. It's already started, you've felt it. The flickering. The bleeding between worlds."

Hunter's hand throbbed. She was right. He had felt it.

The shadow figure slammed the car into reverse, tires screaming. Hunter and Evelyne were thrown against the seats as the sedan shot backward, then forward, barreling out of the parking lot.

"You're not driving fast enough!" Evelyne shouted.

"Faster?" Hunter clung to the grab handle.

They blew past Willow Street. Hunter recognized it. James had bought land there, became obsessed with it for reasons Hunter never understood. Dense woods. Roads that ended abruptly, as if earthmoving machinery had simply stopped mid-job.

The car veered onto a side road. Dirt and gravel exploded beneath the tires. They went airborne for a long moment, Hunter's gut fluttering.

"Are you trying to kill us?" Hunter hollered.

"They're not going fast enough," Evelyne said. "The Rippling is closing."

The vehicle headed straight for a row of trees. Hunter braced for impact.

The interior exploded with white light, blinding. Hunter's eyes burned.

Time fanned out. The light danced, transformed space, made everything disappear.

Hunter saw it, billions of ripples swaying in vastness. Iridescent, colliding with plum-colored light. The sound was overwhelming, every moment of his life happening at once. Tara's laugh, Ember's first cry, his mother's voice calling him home, all layered into a symphony of memory. He tasted copper and ozone and something sweet like burning sugar. The smell of hospital antiseptic mixed with ocean salt mixed with Tara's perfume.

Dark turned to day, day married night, forming black matter. Timelines stacked like windows. Each one a dimension, a possibility, a version of reality where things went differently.

He saw himself dying on Meadow Lane. Saw himself alive. Saw Tara alive. Saw Ember grown. Saw versions where they never existed at all.

This is what I am now. A fixed point. Existing in all timelines at once.

The black matter surrounded him. Not distorting space or time, but providing the catalyst for peeling back windows, revealing what lay beneath. Hunter's bones vibrated. His teeth chattered. The alloy coating his skin pulsed hot, then cold, cycling through temperatures as the timelines bled through him. His skin felt like it was being pulled apart and stitched back together simultaneously, every nerve ending firing.

Hunter gazed at Evelyne. Her face flickered. Tara. Brown eyes became green. Dark hair lightened. His dead wife sat beside him, reaching for his hand.

Then Evelyne again.

Thunder clapped. Hunter's throat went dry, tongue like sandpaper. His lips burst, flooding his mouth with the taste of blood. Black. Red. Black.

He was dying again. Or had never stopped dying. Or would die. All at once.

Then the light bleached everything away, bringing back the world piece by piece. Windows toppling over windows until finally, one window.

The car stood in a vacant alley. The chevrons on his hand pulsed. He covered them with his other palm.

The car moved past the alley, emerging onto a street. An apartment building loomed ahead, brick and stone, elegant bones showing through years of neglect. Black and green stains bleeding from white stone like tears.

But there was something else. Hunter blinked. For just a moment, the building's windows reflected impossible things, rooms that stretched into infinity, galactic corridors that led to other worlds, doors that opened onto timelines. Then it was just brick again. Just a building.

Except it wasn't. Hunter could feel it now, the same pull he'd felt in the Dall. This place existed between realities, a fixed point in the multiverse where all possibilities converged.

A man sat on the weathered bench near the front steps. Older, small, wearing a bright blue sweatband with clothespins fastened to it like headlamps. Clothespins held circular glass lenses in place of sunglasses. Even his shoes were held together with clothespins. The clothespins held everything together—lenses, shoes, what looked like a tear in his jacket sleeve. As if he'd been deconstructed and reconstructed using whatever he could find.

"This place will keep you safe." Evelyne pointed at the man sitting on the bench. "He's your only shot at finding the tablet."

She approached the man. He said something that made her giggle, actually giggle. Hunter felt a spike of jealousy watching them.

Hunter got out of the car and approached.

"You be good, good," the man said to Evelyne.

She smiled. "You too."

"This one work, work?"

"No worse than I was."

He laughed. "We see, see."

She hugged Hunter tight. Her body trembled against his.

Hunter gave her a terrified look. "You can't leave me here."

"I can't stay." Her voice cracked.

Evelyne stared out the window of the car one last time. Her

reflection showed tears sliding down her cheeks, but when Hunter looked at her directly, her face was dry.

"Your reflection is crying," Hunter said.

She didn't turn. "That's the version of me that stays. The one that has to watch you walk away." Her voice dropped to barely a whisper. "In another timeline, I'm the one holding that Jar, erasing myself to save you. In another, I never met you at all. Every version of me makes different choices, and every version lives with the consequences." She finally looked at him. "This version gets to say goodbye. That's something."

She got in the car. It sped off.

Hunter stood alone on the street, watching the taillights disappear. His hands were shaking. Not from the chevrons, not from the transformation, from everything else. Tara was dead. Evelyne was gone. That green-eyed woman who looked at him like he was her whole world was a stranger he couldn't remember. His life had splintered into pieces he couldn't put back together, and now he was supposed to trust a man wearing clothespins as glasses to help him find some tablet that might save... what, exactly? He didn't even know anymore. He just knew he had to keep moving, because stopping meant thinking, and thinking meant breaking.

The man, Hugo, stared at him through those dark clothespin lenses.

"Let's go, go. We have no time, time."

Hugo bumped past him, heading for the building's entrance. His small stature somehow commanded authority. "Come, come."

Hunter followed, casting one last look at where Evelyne's car had disappeared.

Pain throbbed through his hand. He looked down. The chevrons were there, covering his entire palm now, pulsing in rhythm with his heartbeat. Then gone.

I'm running out of time.

Hugo held open the ornate iron door. "This way, way." He paused, meeting Hunter's eyes through those dark lenses. "Never come this way, way. Only one time, time. Okay, okay?"

Hunter said nothing.

Hugo examined him through those dark clothespin lenses. For a moment, the old man's posture shifted, became taller, more formidable. His voice lost its stutter. "No, you will return." Then the stutter crept back. "I see, see. Seven times, Hunter." The voice dropped again, clear and ancient. "Seven times you enter. Seven times you fail. But the seventh—" He stopped, shook his head, and the stutter returned fully. "No, no. Cannot say, say. Knowing changes, changes."

Hunter's blood ran cold. "Seven times? What happens the seventh time?"

"Everything, everything." Hugo turned away. "Or nothing, nothing."

Hugo disappeared into the building. Hunter looked back at the empty street one more time. At the bench where Hugo had been sitting. At the alley. At the watch in his pocket, frozen at three-thirty-three.

Thunder rolled. The building flickered. For a moment, it was glass and crystal, the Dall. Then brick again.

Hunter took a breath and stepped through the door.

It sealed behind him with a wet thud, the same wet thud as the Dall, when he killed the Time Recorder.

The grand alien corridor stretched before him, impossibly long. Wallpaper peeled in strips, revealing brick beneath. Or was it crystal? Hunter blinked. Brick again. The air smelled of mildew and something else, ozone. The Dall's signature.

This place exists between worlds, he realized. Just like me.

"Come, come!" Hugo's voice echoed from somewhere ahead, layered with harmonics that shouldn't exist.

Hunter followed the sound into the depths of the building, leaving the sunlit street behind. The door sealed with finality, and somewhere in the darkness ahead, Hugo waited.

Along with whatever doom he'd prophesied.

Seven times.

The number echoed in Hunter's mind as he descended into shadow.

part twelve
the smith sisters

Nick's hands wouldn't stop shaking. He had escorted diplomats, weapons manufacturers, and billionaires who thought they owned the world, but none had rattled him like the Smith sisters. Their identical wool suits, identical wine-colored pocket squares, and identical creepy smiles that never reached their eyes moved through the office like panthers sizing up their next meal.

Their matching heels clicked in perfect synchronization, not quite human timing. Too precise, and nearly mechanical.

As they passed, Nick caught a scent, ozone and something else. Burnt copper, as though lightning had struck inside the building. The smell clung to them like radiation.

"Those socks are bright." The taller one, Ms. Smith, said, though both claimed that name. They studied his ankles with a stare that made his scalp prickle. "Something a child would choose?"

Nick stopped walking. He'd worked here for twelve years, weathered every kind of corporate intimidation. But something about her tone, the way she had emphasized the word child, made goosebumps spread across the back of his neck.

He forced himself to meet her gaze. "It's casual Friday."

"Refreshing." Her lips peeled back, revealing teeth as uniform as piano keys.

Did you see his reaction?

Nick couldn't hear the thought, but he felt it. Warmth spread behind his eyes, like someone had opened a door in his skull and peered inside. He blinked hard, pulse burning in his throat.

"Right this way." He walked faster, the certainty thrashing through him that something deadly followed.

They passed through cubicles, phones ringing, keyboards clicking, conversations about quarterly projections, but the usual office sounds felt fragile now. Breakable, in that eerie way where everything might collapse if the Smith sisters simply chose to snap their bony fingers.

When they finally reached the conference room, Nick had to force himself not to sprint. "Ms. Rosenberg, this is Ms. and Ms. Smith."

Evelyne faced the glass walls stretching floor to ceiling, silhouetted against Central Park's sprawling green. She didn't turn around immediately. "Please come in. Make yourselves comfortable."

There was tension in her voice. Nick recognized it because he felt it too. He met her gaze, trying to communicate the wrongness of these women without words. Evelyne's expression shifted, reading him. For just a moment, Nick thought he saw something flicker in her eyes, a violet shimmer, like heat lightning behind storm clouds. He blinked. Her eyes were brown again.

"Message Mr. Lewis to stand by." She turned to glance at Nick and the sisters. "I may need his help in a few minutes."

"Yes, Ms. Rosenberg." Nick's fingers twitched toward his tablet. "I can wait in the hallway, in case you need anything else."

"That won't be necessary." Her tone left no room for argument.

The door slid shut behind him with a gentle chime that sounded too much like a coffin closing.

Evelyne watched the women's reflection in the glass as they struggled with the executive chairs, wheeling around briefly before settling. Their movements were too stiff, too deliberate, as though they were puppets operated by someone who'd only read about humans in a manual.

She'd reviewed their proposal with the board three times. The valuation was insulting. The terms were predatory. And the fact that they'd insisted on this meeting despite already receiving her rejection meant they didn't intend to take no for an answer.

"Shall we get right to business?" Evelyne kept her position at the window, maintaining distance.

If Hunter were here, he'd tell her to stay anchored, keep the high ground. The memory of his face, not Tara's husband, but hers, from a timeline that didn't exist yet, flashed through her mind. The way he'd kissed her in that moment between worlds, not knowing who she really was. She shoved the thought down and focused.

"I've reviewed your proposal with the board. After serious consideration, we've decided this partnership is not in the best interests of McDermott & Persefoni." She turned to face them. "Your valuation is considerably low, and you're requesting sole interest in our nano company. We're rejecting your offer."

"She refuses to listen." The taller Smith sister shot a glance at her partner, blank-faced.

"Humans rarely comprehend on the first attempt." The partner tilted her head, studying Evelyne like a spider under glass. "Patience. She will reconsider. They always do."

Evelyne stepped closer, gripping the back of a chair. The leather was cold under her palms. "There is no deal."

The taller Smith sister's stare intensified, pupils dilating impossibly wide. Evelyne felt warmth push against her mind, gentle, invasive, like fingers probing the edges of her consciousness. She stepped back, flooding her thoughts with images of the park below. Trees. Birds. Butterflies. Hunter's hands holding hers.

"You insisted on this meeting." Evelyne's voice came out steadier than she felt. "You knew our decision beforehand. The board has made its decision."

"We had hoped you were the reasonable one." The tall Smith sister's accent thickened, consonants curling around her teeth with a slithery undertone. "That you possessed adequate self-preservation instincts."

Evelyne turned back to the window and met her own gaze in the glass. "I've survived worse than corporate espionage from amateurs in matching suits." She held her ground, though every instinct screamed at her to back away.

The partner laughed, sharp, brittle, like glass breaking. "Enlighten us, Ms. Rosenberg. What do you believe you know?"

Evelyne moved toward the door. "I'm confident you can find your way out."

"I predicted her refusal." The partner's fingers drummed the table with inhuman rhythm.

"We are not finished, Ms. Rosenberg." The tall Smith sister leaned across the table, and the conference room temperature dropped. Evelyne's breath misted. Ice crystallized along her collarbone, her fingers numbing against the chair. "We do not require your permission. Our visit was merely procedural courtesy." She stepped closer. "Your corporation behaves as a foolish primate clutching godlike powers. This cannot be permitted to continue."

Evelyne's jaw tightened. "I don't quite follow."

"I believe you comprehend perfectly." The partner's gaze locked onto hers, red, iridescent, spinning like galaxies collapsing into singularities.

The Smith sisters rose, synchronized, grins splitting across their faces like cracked porcelain. "Oh, Ms. Rosenberg." The tall Smith's voice layered with harmonics that shouldn't exist in human vocal cords. "You have committed a grave error. But it is inconsequential. In mere moments, you will remember nothing."

Evelyne held the Smith sisters' stare, and her pulse thrashed.

The tall Smith sister's eyes matched her partner's. Both women stared with hypnotic intensity, pupils dilating and contracting in synchronized rhythm. Their grins stretched wider. Skin melted, reformed, melted again like wax under flame. The air between them shimmered, warped, bent like heat over asphalt.

The burnt copper smell intensified, scorching the back of Evelyne's throat.

Evelyne felt it immediately, warmth spreading behind her forehead, then pressure. Like hands squeezing her skull. Forget the meeting. The words weren't hers. They slithered through her thoughts like oil spreading across water.

The board meeting from yesterday dissolved first. She'd been presenting something important, what was it? The faces around the mahogany table blurred into watercolor smears. Her assistant's name slipped away like sand through fingers. What had she eaten for breakfast? Coffee tasted like static on her tongue, the memory glitching around the edges.

Sign the contract.

Her vision blurred. The sisters' faces multiplied, fractured like reflections in broken mirrors. What were they discussing? The room tilted. She grabbed the chair for balance, knuckles bloodless. Even her own name felt foreign in her mind, letters rearranging themselves into meaningless symbols.

Give us the company.

Hunter's face flickered in her memory. His hand touching her cheek, his lips on hers in that moment between worlds, the impossible recognition in his eyes. Then it started to fade, dissolving like blood in rain. She watched the memory drain away, pixel by pixel, until only darkness remained.

No.

Something inside her ignited. Not a thought, but a force, ancient, protective, furious. The invasion hit a wall and shattered. The alien voices scattered like startled birds. The pressure evaporated. Hunter's face sharpened back into focus, more vivid than before. The board meeting reconstructed itself. Her memories flooded back in a rush that made her gasp.

Evelyne blinked. The Smith sisters were still staring, eyes glowing like headlights in fog. But their expressions had shifted, confusion bleeding through their control.

"That's..." The tall Smith sister's gaze intensified, light brightening until Evelyne had to squint. "Not possible."

The executive chair scraped across the floor. "She is protected."

"By what mechanism?" The tall Smith sister's voice cracked upward, accent fracturing. "How does she—"

Evelyne straightened, releasing the chair. Her hands steadied. Whatever had defended her, the nano technology dormant in her bloodstream, some quantum entanglement with Hunter across timelines, or something else entirely, she didn't know. But she could feel it humming beneath her skin now, warm and certain.

"I have a tight schedule to keep," she said. "Please find the door."

The Smith sisters exchanged a glance. The first genuine emotion Evelyne had seen from them. Fear.

"You have purchased yourself time." The tall Smith sister's eyes dimmed, returning to something approximating human. "We arrived offering partnership. Now..." She smoothed her suit with mechanical precision. "Catastrophic accidents occur in buildings this tall. Wouldn't it be unfortunate if your nano patents fell into unauthorized hands during a... security breach?"

"Are you threatening me?"

"We are clarifying the consequences." The partner moved toward the door, the tall Smith following in lockstep. "The board votes on releasing nano technology to the public in forty-eight hours. Much can change in two days. Many individuals can alter their positions." She paused at the threshold, face resetting into that pleasant mask. "Or cease to exist entirely."

They left without another word, heels clicking in perfect rhythm down the hall.

Evelyne waited until the sound faded, then her legs gave out. She sank into the chair, breath coming in shallow gasps. Her palms had left sweat marks on the leather armrest. She pressed her fingers to her temples, checking for damage, for gaps in her memory. Everything was intact. Somehow.

She stood on trembling legs, steadied herself against the table, and straightened her suit jacket. Her reflection in the window glass looked pale but composed. Professional. She smoothed her hair back, erasing any evidence of what had just happened.

The door opened. Nick stood there, face pale. "Ms. Rosenberg? Are you—"

"Get me Mr. Lewis." Evelyne's voice cracked. She cleared her throat, forced steel back into it. "And find out where Hunter is."

"Is everything—"

"They tried to erase my memory, Nick." She looked up at him, and for the first time in twelve years, Nick saw genuine fear in her eyes. "If they come back..." She swallowed hard. "Find Hunter. Now."

Nick nodded and fled.

Evelyne walked back to the window on steadying legs. The storm had arrived, rain lashing the glass, thunder rolling across the park. Whatever protection kept her immune to their mind control, she needed to understand it. Before they came back. Before the board vote. Before they decided to stop asking permission.

She pressed her palm against the cold glass. Lightning forked across the sky, illuminating her reflection, and for just a moment, she could have sworn her eyes flashed purple. She blinked. They were brown again.

She didn't know what was happening to her, but she would find out before they returned.

Outside, rain trickled down the windows toward the street below.

part thirteen
the sacrifice

The elevator doors closed on the Smith sisters. Evelyne's heart thrashed beneath her ribs. Forty-eight hours. That's all she had before the board vote, before they came back with an army instead of threats.

She pulled out her phone. Her finger hovered over Hunter's contact, then moved past it. He was fighting his own war in the Dall, becoming something she wasn't sure she'd recognize. Calling him now would only distract him from surviving.

Evelyne walked back to the conference room and stared out at Central Park. Somewhere in that expanse of green, her daughter was waiting for the signal. The signal that meant Evelyne had made her choice. Her gaze swept across the landscape, lingering on Bow Bridge arching gracefully over the water. The bridge where Hunter had once said she looked like she'd been waiting her whole life. She had been.

Her reflection stared back from the cold glass. Eyes that had once been human, now burning with something else. Something the aliens had created but couldn't control.

"I'm sorry, baby," she whispered to the city below. Her fingers gripped the window frame so hard her knuckles cracked, white bone pressing against translucent skin. "But your father needs more time."

She turned from the window and walked to her office. Time to set the trap. The safe was hidden behind a bronze panel in her private office, a room most employees avoided. The Dall's alloy coating gave the space an otherworldly quality, like stepping inside a crystal. Some said it appeared overnight. Others claimed it had always been there, just invisible until Evelyne needed it. Both were true, in a sense.

She pressed her palm to the panel. It liquefied, revealing an alabaster column rising from the floor. Nestled at the top sat the Jar. The device was no larger than her fist, a crystal sphere with edges sharp enough to cut skin.

James McDermott had warned her the day he gave it to her. She could still see him, skin translucent as wax paper, veins glowing faintly beneath like radioactive rivers mapped across dying flesh. His jaw hung loose where the bone had deteriorated, words slurring through the gap. Death already clawing at his throat.

"Last resort only." His voice had faded to a gurgle, lungs failing. "Nothing that enters the Jar ever comes back. Not the aliens. Not the building." He had gripped her wrist, fingers cold as winter. "Not you."

Evelyne lifted the sphere carefully. It clung to the column for a moment, as if the Dall itself refused to release it. She pulled harder, and it came free with a sound like tearing silk. The Jar throbbed in her palm, sensing her touch, warming to body temperature. Light fractured through its depths. Black matter that shouldn't exist. Light that consumed rather than illuminated. She turned it slowly, watching colors ripple across its surface like pathogens smashed between microscope slides.

The nanites in her bloodstream carried temporal signatures from seventeen different timelines. If that wasn't authority, nothing was. The Jar would recognize her command, even if it needed the Time Keeper's voice to complete the activation.

"Last resort it is."

Evelyne's hands trembled as she left her office, the Jar burning a hole in her pocket.

"Becky." Her voice came out too quiet. She cleared her throat, tried again. "Becky! Initiate evacuation protocol."

Her assistant looked up, and whatever she saw in Evelyne's face made her go pale. "Ms. Rosenberg."

"Everyone out. Twenty minutes." Evelyne forced steel into her voice even as her pulse thrashed. "The Smith sisters are coming back. And they're bringing an army."

Becky's fingers flew to her keyboard, then froze. "If I activate the protocol, the entire network locks down. It could take months to restore."

"I know." Evelyne leaned over the desk, gripping the edge to keep her hands steady. "Do it anyway. The nano company cannot fall into their hands."

Becky stared at her for a long moment, reading between the lines, understanding what Evelyne wasn't saying. "What's the passphrase?"

"All caps. 'Infect the original host.'"

Becky typed, hands trembling. The cursor hovered over the activate key.

"Do it."

Becky hit enter.

Every alarm in the building wailed to life. Screens flashed red. Emergency lights strobed. The building's AI voice echoed through the halls on repeat: Contamination detected. Evacuate immediately.

Then the phones started ringing. One. Ten. Hundreds. A cascading symphony of panic as the network locked down, wiping decades of research in seconds. Evelyne watched employees flood from their offices in controlled chaos, confusion and fear etched on their faces.

Becky grabbed her backpack, stuffing belongings inside. She stood, then hesitated, finger hovering over the elevator button. She looked back.

"You're not coming, are you?"

Evelyne turned away before Becky could see her eyes welling. "Don't look back. Don't make this harder."

"Ms. Rosenberg."

"Go." Evelyne's voice cracked.

Becky's tears came then, silent and streaming. She pressed a sticky note into Evelyne's hand. "Lieutenant Williams called during your meeting. He demanded Mr. Persefoni's address." Her voice dropped to a whisper. "I didn't give it to him. But if something happens to you."

"Give him this." Evelyne scribbled on the note. "Tell him Evelyne says it starts now."

Then Becky was gone, swept into the tide of evacuating employees. The elevator doors closed on her tear-stained face.

Evelyne stood alone in the reception area, watching the exodus through the glass walls. Two hundred people flooded onto the sidewalk below, tiny as ants from this height.

She'd staged the remodel weeks ago, cleared out most of the building's floors to reduce casualties when this moment came. Because she'd always known it would come.

The executive floor fell silent except for the wailing alarms and the strobe lights painting everything red and blue. Evelyne walked to her desk and opened the bottom drawer. Photos. Solenne at age five, gap-toothed and laughing. Hunter from timeline Echo-7, the first divergence point, before he knew her name. A team photo from the nano company launch, back when they'd thought they were saving the world.

She closed the drawer. Checked her watch. Fifteen minutes since evacuation began. The aliens would come soon. They always came when you were most alone.

One last call. One last goodbye. She pressed Solenne's contact. It connected immediately.

"Mom?" Her daughter's voice was tight with fear. "Is it time?"

"Yes." Evelyne walked back to the conference room, phone pressed to her ear. "Are you in position?"

"I'm in the alley across from your building. I can see the evacuation from here." A soft sniffle rose through the line. "You don't have to do this. We can run. The portal network in Prague is still secure. Uncle Silas has the backup facility in—"

"Not this time, baby." Evelyne stopped at the window, staring out at the park glowing beneath the eye of the storm. A strange calm too sharp to trust. "Your father needs time. The nanites are still integrating with his system. The chevrons." Her voice caught. "If they find him before the transformation completes, he won't survive. And if he doesn't survive, none of us do."

"Then let me help you. I can portal in, we can fight them together, we can—"

"No." The word came out harder than intended. Evelyne softened her tone. "You have to stay hidden. You promised me you'd stop sacrificing yourself. You promised."

Silence. Then Solenne's voice, small and broken, "You promised first. Years ago. You said you'd stop playing martyr."

Evelyne pressed her forehead against the cold glass until it ached. "I know. I'm sorry. But I'm not being a martyr this time. I'm being strategic." She pressed her fingers to the glass. "Hunter would call this martyrdom. You'd call it abandonment. But I call it the only choice left. Promise me when this is over, you'll find your father. You tell him who I was. Who we are to him." Her voice dropped to a whisper. "Tell him I loved him in every timeline. Even the ones where he didn't know me."

Silence on the other end. Then, quietly, "I promise."

Beyond her reflection, the park glowed. Trees swaying, umbrellas bobbing, people outrunning the rain, a world that would never know what she was about to do.

"I love you, baby."

"Mom, wait—"

"I'll find a way back."

"I love you."

The call ended.

Evelyne lowered the phone. Pulled the Jar from her pocket. Placed it on the conference table. Heat spiked through her palm, the Jar's fail-safe, testing her resolve one final time. She didn't flinch.

"Activate Jar," she said, voice quivering as she held back the tears. "Contain perimeter, including host Evelyne. Activate on the Time Keeper's authority."

The sphere pulsed once, waiting.

Now all she had to do was survive long enough to trigger it.

The silence stretched. Five minutes. Ten. Evelyne stood alone in the empty building, surrounded by strobing lights and wailing alarms. She checked her watch. Her reflection in the dark screen looked pale, haunted.

The burnt copper smell hit her first. Then the elevator chimed. Once. Twice. Three times in rapid succession.

Evelyne turned from the window as the Smith sisters and the Time Keeper stepped into the reception area. A dozen more Ouroboros filled the space behind them, skin flickering between human suits and something reptilian beneath. The ozone scent flooded the floor, so thick Evelyne could taste it on her tongue. Metal and lightning and ancient rot.

"Isolation." The Time Keeper's voice was cold, analytical. It circled the empty space, clawed fingers trailing across abandoned desks. "Proactive. Foolish. She believes solitude will preserve her."

The tall Smith sister's eyes flashed red. "They fragment so predictably, these fixed points. Like crystalline structures under pressure, beautiful, inevitable."

Evelyne stepped forward, spine straight. "I've sat through hostile takeovers. Government indictments. Death threats from people far scarier than you." Her voice was ice. "You think I'm afraid of reptiles in suits?"

The Time Keeper circled slowly, flanked by its soldiers. Evelyne counted fifteen, twenty, thirty. An army.

"You should have brought more."

"How pitiable, this human attachment." The Time Keeper gestured to the empty office with disdain. "The weapon mourning her creators."

"A weapon that will be your extinction." Evelyne's lips curved into something that wasn't quite a smile. "Consider this my final offer."

The tall Smith sister took a step forward, but the Time Keeper blocked her. "Patience. She will fracture soon enough." It studied Evelyne with ancient eyes that had watched civilizations rise and fall. "Bravo, Ms. Rosenberg. You've solved the riddle. Now we will extract payment for your cleverness."

More of them poured into the conference room. An invasion, not a negotiation. Evelyne closed her eyes briefly, savored one last memory. Hunter's face, Solenne's laugh, the smell of rain in the park, that bench at Bow Bridge where he'd seen through every timeline to the truth of her.

Then she opened her eyes and smiled. "I have something for you."

The Time Keeper tilted its head, curiosity flickering across its features. "What could you possibly possess that I require?"

"A relic." Evelyne gestured to the Jar sitting on the table. "I think you might recognize it."

The aliens pressed closer, but the Time Keeper held up one clawed hand. Its eyes narrowed, pupils contracting to vertical slits. "You expect us to believe you would simply relinquish a powerful weapon?"

Evelyne's heart hammered, but she kept her face blank. "Not a weapon. A prison. For your enemies. The Synods created it to contain fixed points when they became... problematic." She let that word hang in the air. "I thought you might appreciate the irony."

The Time Keeper circled the table slowly, studying the Jar from every angle. Light refracted through the crystal, casting twisted shadows across its reptilian features. "How does it function?"

"Verbal command. From someone with temporal authority." Evelyne forced herself to breathe slowly. "I tried to activate it myself, but —" She gestured to her strange-colored eyes. "I'm just a weapon. It won't respond to me."

The tall Smith reached for the sphere, but the Time Keeper blocked her. "Wait."

Evelyne's pulse thrashed. She needed to push harder. "Unless you're afraid?" She let contempt creep into her voice. "The great Time Keeper, terrified of a device built by your own kind?"

The Time Keeper's eyes flashed red with wounded pride and ancient fury. It placed one clawed on the sphere. "What is the command?"

Evelyne met its gaze. "Activate Jar."

For a long moment, the Time Keeper stared at her, searching for the lie, probing for the trap. Then its smile widened, revealing rows of serrated teeth. "Activate Jar."

The sphere cracked open.

Not with sound, but with its absence. A void where sound should be, silence so complete it felt like pressure against her eardrums. Black light erupted in all directions, and Evelyne felt the temperature plummet. Her breath frosted. Her teeth chattered. Frost crystallized in her eyelashes. The air turned thick, viscous, like wading through oil.

Tendrils of darkness wrapped around the nearest Ouroboros. It screamed, a sound that cut off mid-note as the light consumed it. Not burned. Not killed. Erased. Its body flickered once, twice, then ceased to exist, as if reality had simply forgotten it had ever been born.

The other aliens scrambled backward, clawing over each other in primal terror, but the tendrils moved faster. They raced across the floor, up the walls, through the ceiling. Wherever they touched, matter dissolved into black mist. The building shuddered. Cracks spiderwebbed across the windows. The park view fractured like a broken mirror, reality itself shattering.

An Ouroboros tried to escape through a wall. The black light caught it halfway, body phasing through plaster and steel. It hung there, suspended between dimensions, mouth open in silent agony. Its hand remained visible for a moment, five clawed fingers grasping at nothing, before that too vanished.

Another turned to face Evelyne, eyes wide with shock and terror. You did this. The thought blazed between them before the creature dissolved, erased mid-scream.

"You imbecilic—"

The black light wrapped around the Time Keeper's throat, cutting off the words. Its eyes widened in horror, perhaps the first genuine surprise it had felt in millennia. It opened its mouth, but nothing emerged except a frequency that made Evelyne's bones vibrate. Windows shattered. Light fixtures exploded. The air itself seemed to tear, ripping through the fabric of reality like cloth.

The black light caught the tall Smith sister mid-leap. The alien hung suspended, half-real, half-erased, body flickering like a corrupted hologram. Her face stretched in terror, mouth forming words that would never be spoken. Then she vanished completely, leaving only the faint scent of ozone.

Evelyne pressed her back against the window, watching the devastation spread. The black light raced through walls, through floors, consuming steel and glass and flesh without distinction or mercy.

"You asked once if I'd trade my life for theirs." Evelyne's voice was steady despite the chaos, despite the cold numbing her fingers. "I already answered that question."

The building groaned, a sound like the earth splitting open. Reality bent around the Jar's power, spacetime folding in on itself.

Evelyne closed her eyes and reached for her favorite memory. Not the park. Not the office. That moment five years ago, timeline Echo-7, the first divergence point, before everything went wrong.

Hunter had taken her to the park on their first date, not knowing she'd traveled decades to find him. Solenne wasn't born yet. The Ouroboros didn't know fixed points existed. They'd sat on that bench near Bow Bridge, and Hunter had said, "You look like you've been waiting your whole life for this moment."

And she had. Across seventeen timelines, through countless variations of their story, she'd been waiting for him to see her.

The black light wrapped around her like a shroud. Ice crystallized along her collarbone. She felt herself dissolving, not into nothing, but into everywhere. Scattered across timelines, across possibilities, across every version of the story where she'd loved him.

Find him, Solenne. Tell him I never stopped waiting.

Then the Jar consumed her, and Evelyne Rosenberg ceased to exist.

The building vanished.

One moment, McDermott & Persefoni's headquarters towered forty stories above the street. The next, nothing remained but an empty lot. Not rubble. Not ash. Just absence.

Where skyscraper and steel had stood, grass now carpeted the ground—impossible grass, too green, too perfect, as if the Dall had claimed the space immediately. Cracked pavement showed through in places where reality hadn't quite decided what belonged there. The foundation remained visible, concrete edges marking where the building had rooted itself into Manhattan bedrock.

Pedestrians stopped mid-stride, staring. Cars screeched to a halt. Someone screamed.

But there was no explosion. No rubble. No bodies. Just emptiness where something massive had been.

A man in a business suit pulled out his phone, filming. "Must've been a controlled demolition," he said to his companion, voice shaking. "Weird they didn't warn anyone."

His companion stared at the grass pushing through impossible cracks. "That's not how demolitions work."

But the man was already typing, crafting a mundane explanation for the cosmic horror he'd witnessed. The mind protecting itself from truths it couldn't process.

In the center of the lot, the Jar sat gleaming. A crystal sphere reflecting the dying sunlight.

Solenne materialized in the alley facing the grassy lot. Tears streamed down her face. She had watched through the portal as the black light consumed everything. Watched her mother stand unflinching as it erased her from existence. Watched the building fold in on itself, collapse into a singularity, and disappear.

"She actually did it."

Solenne stepped out of the alley's shadow. Pedestrians rushed past her, phones out, filming the empty lot, crafting explanations, protecting themselves from truth. No one noticed the girl walking calmly toward the grass, toward the gleaming sphere at its center.

She knelt and picked up the Jar. The moment her fingers touched the crystal, she felt it, her mother's last thought. Not words but pure emotion. Worth it.

The Jar was warm, still pulsing with residual energy. Inside its crystalline depths, she could see shapes moving, shadows of the aliens trapped in its prison, existing and not existing simultaneously. And there, at the center, a flicker of green light. Her mother's eyes, still watching. Still protecting.

"The world will never know." Solenne's voice broke.

A sharp pain lanced through her chest. She pressed her fist against her heart, trying to hold herself together. "I know. And he'll know too. That's all that matters now."

Her legs gave out. She collapsed onto the grass, Jar clutched to her chest. Her scream split the evening air, raw and animal, the sound of a daughter who'd watched her mother choose annihilation. Sirens wailed in the distance, but she couldn't move. Couldn't breathe. Her mother was gone. Really, truly gone. Not just dead, erased from existence. From every timeline. From every possibility.

No one should die alone like that.

But Evelyne hadn't been alone. She'd been surrounded by enemies she'd trapped with her. Defiant to the last second.

Solenne pressed her forehead to the cold sphere. Let herself break. Just for a moment. Pedestrians gave her wide berth, assuming grief for something mundane, a breakup, a job loss, anything but the truth.

Then she stood. Wiped her eyes. The Dall was waiting. Hunter was waiting.

"I'm coming, Dad," she said quietly. "And you're not going to like what I have to tell you."

She closed her eyes and summoned the portal, gold sparkles, starlight, the familiar pull of home. The Dall was waiting. Hunter was waiting, though he didn't know it yet. Didn't know what had been sacrificed to keep him alive.

The portal opened, brilliant and blinding. Solenne stepped through, the Jar secure in her jacket, her mother's last light pressed against her heart.

Behind her, the lot lay empty except for the grass swaying in the evening breeze and the businessmen filming, already crafting their comfortable lies. A monument to a sacrifice the world would never understand, explained away as construction, as government secrecy, as anything but what it was.

A mother's love, scattered across infinite timelines.

A weapon that chose to save rather than destroy.

A sacrifice that would echo through every reality where her family still breathed.

part fourteen
fixed point

Hunter stopped walking. "No."

Hugo turned, those clothespin lenses reflecting nothing. "No, no?"

"No more riddles." Hunter straightened, feeling the chevrons pulse beneath his skin. "Where's the tablet?"

"But you need to understand, understand—"

"I understand enough." Hunter pushed past him. "Evelyne sacrificed herself. My daughter is out there somewhere. The Ouroboros are hunting me. I'm running out of time." He grabbed Hugo's collar, snapping away a clothespin. "Show me where it is, or I'll knock your teeth in."

Hugo stared at him. Then the old man's posture shifted, becoming taller, more formidable. His voice lost its stutter completely. "Good. I was beginning to think you'd never demand anything for yourself."

"No more tests," Hunter pulled him closer, more clothespins snapping away. "No more bullshit, show me."

"The tablet doesn't respond to the passive, Hunter. It requires will. Choice." Hugo's face remained unchanged, but his presence filled the strange corridor. "It's been waiting for you, but you have to fight for your future. You have to be damn sure, or else."

He moved fast, but Hunter matched his pace. The strange corridor opened into a white room, pure white, infinite space. Ocean breeze filled the air, mixing with distant, salty waves. In the center, a pedestal. On top, the tablet. Hunter didn't wait for permission. He crossed the room in five strides and grabbed it. Reality exploded. The visions slammed into him, Flying Point Road, the Dall, Williams' interrogation room, but Hunter pushed through them, searching. Show me Solenne.

The tablet responded. The visions shifted. Central Park. A woman, Evelyne, but younger. Happier. She held a baby with green eyes.

"Solenne," Evelyne said, smiling at him. A version of him that had chosen differently, lived differently.

"Our daughter."

Hunter watched himself in that timeline. Watched the family he had built. Solenne's first steps on the Great Lawn. Teaching her to read beneath Bow Bridge. Her fifth birthday at the natural history museum, staring up at the blue whale with those green eyes, his eyes, full of wonder.

A life. A whole life he'd never lived.

Then he watched it collapse. Saw himself at Flying Point Road in that timeline too, saw the moment he called out across every reality, begging for power to stop death, to save everyone. Saw the universe answer by making him a fixed point. Saw that timeline fracture like glass.

Evelyne screaming as reality folded in on itself. Solenne, his daughter, his little girl, ripped away as the timelines separated. And Evelyne makes the choice, sacrificing herself to give Solenne a chance to survive in another timeline. A timeline where Hunter had never met Evelyne. Where Tara existed instead. Where everything was different.

The vision showed Evelyne standing in a conference room surrounded by Ouroboros. The Jar activating. Black light consuming everything. The building disappearing. And Solenne, seven years old, alone, materializing in an empty lot, picking up the crystal sphere with her mother trapped inside, tears streaming down her face.

"Mom? Mom, can you hear me?"

The little girl pressed her face against the Jar, trying to reach the woman trapped within. Evelyne's hand against the crystal from inside, pressing back. Both crying.

"I'm here, baby. I'm still here."

"I'm scared."

"You have to be brave. For me. For your father. He's out there somewhere, and he doesn't remember us yet. You have to find him. Help him become what he needs to be. Can you do that?"

The little girl nodded, clutching the Jar. "I promise."

Hunter watched Solenne grow up across timelines. Watched her hunt for him. Watched her fail, again and again, across countless realities. Watched her never give up. Watched her become the woman in the pilot's cap, standing at that train station, staring at him through car window glass with heartbreak in her eyes when he didn't recognize her. All of it to save him. All of it because Evelyne had sacrificed everything to give their daughter a chance.

"Show me how to save them both."

The tablet went dark. Then showed him one image, himself, fully transformed, chevrons covering every inch. A fixed point. Eternal. Inhuman. Alone forever.

"No." Hunter's voice cracked. "There has to be another way."

The tablet pulsed. Showed him the alternative, dissolution. His consciousness scattering across infinite timelines, existing everywhere and nowhere until there was nothing left of who he'd been.

"Those are both death sentences."

The tablet didn't answer. It liquefied, merging with the alloy coating his skin, embedding itself in his palm. Hunter gasped as the device integrated. The chevrons exploded across his body, up his chest, across his shoulders, climbing his neck. He could feel them locking into place. Permanent now.

He fell to his knees. The weight of all timelines pressed down on him simultaneously. He could feel every version of himself. The one who lived with Tara, the one who lived with Evelyne, the one who saved Ember, the one who lost her, the one who never existed at all. All of them screaming. All of them dying. All of them trapped inside his fracturing mind.

"I can't—" Hunter's hands clawed at the white floor. "It's too much. I can see everything. Every choice. Every failure. Every—"

Thunder cracked outside. Hunter's head snapped up. Through the white walls, somehow transparent now, he saw her. Solenne. Materializing in gold light on the street, older now, seventeen maybe. The Jar clutched to her chest. Her pilot's cap askew. Lifetimes of exhaustion and pain etched on her young face. Their eyes met across impossible distance. Recognition flashed in her expression. Relief. Terror. Hope crashing into despair.

She started running toward the building. Hunter staggered to his feet. His legs barely worked. The tablet's integration had left him weak, trembling, bleeding from his nose. Black drops turning red, then black again. But he forced himself forward.

"She's here," he whispered.

"Always, always," Hugo said quietly, his stutter returning. "She never stopped, stopped. Never gave up, up."

Hunter crashed through doors, following his daughter's presence. The building's impossible architecture shifted around him, but he didn't care. He turned corners, descended stairs, moved on instinct. And then he saw her. Solenne stood at the end of the alien corridor. Smaller than he had imagined. Younger. Her pilot's cap covered dark hair. The Jar pulsed against her chest. She was shaking.

They stared at each other. Father and daughter. Strangers and family. Separated by timelines and choices and cosmic horror that had stolen everything from both of them.

"Dad?" Solenne's voice broke on the word, uncertain, like she was afraid he still wouldn't

remember. "Do you... do you know me now?"

Hunter felt cold tears streaming down his face. Inky machine tears. The chevrons pulsed brighter across his scaled skin, responding to emotion he thought the transformation had stolen.

"Solenne." His voice cracked. "My little girl. I remember. I remember everything. Central Park. The blue whale. Your fifth birthday. Teaching you to read. I remember—" His legs gave out. He collapsed to his knees. "I'm sorry. God, I'm so sorry I didn't remember you. That I forgot—"

"It's okay." She took a step forward. Then another. Tears streamed down her face too. "You're remembering now. That's what matters."

She closed the distance between them. Knelt beside him. Her small hand reached out, touched his scaled cheek. She flinched at the texture but didn't pull away.

"Your face," she whispered. "What did they do to you?"

"I became what I needed to be." Hunter covered her hand with his, scales rough against her soft skin. "To find you. To save you."

"You don't have to save me, Dad. I'm supposed to save you. That's what Mom said. That's why she—" Solenne's voice broke. She held up the Jar. Inside, Evelyne's face pressed against the crystal, watching them. Still beautiful. Still fierce. Still his wife from another life.

Hunter took the Jar with trembling hands. The moment his scaled fingers touched the crystal, warmth flooded through him. Not heat, connection. He could feel Evelyne inside, her consciousness still intact despite the prison.

"Hunter." Her voice dissolved in his mind. Soft and loving. The voice he'd heard in the vision saying his name across morning coffee, across dinner tables, across whispered conversations in the dark.

I'm here, he thought back. I found her. Our daughter. She's safe.

I know. I've been watching. Through the Jar, I can see her. See you. A pause, You look terrible.

Despite everything, Hunter almost laughed. I became a monster.

You became what you needed to be. That's not the same thing. Evelyne's presence strengthened. Hunter, listen. The tablet showed you two choices, but there's a third. It's dangerous. It might not work. But if you're willing to risk everything—

Tell me.

Don't use the tablet to stabilize yourself. Use it to destabilize the Ouroboros. They're connected across all timelines, just like you. But unlike you, they're machines. No humanity left. No emotion. That's their weakness. How is that a weakness?

Because you still feel. You still love. That's what makes you different. What makes you stronger? Her voice dropped to a whisper. Use that love as a weapon. Show them what they gave up when they became eternal. Make them remember what it means to lose everything.

That will kill me.

Maybe. Or maybe it will transform you into something new.

Something neither human nor Ouroboros. A pause. Either way, our daughter will be safe. That's all that matters.

Hunter pulled his hand back. Looked at Solenne kneeling beside him, her green eyes, his eyes, Evelyne's eyes, staring up at him with desperate hope.

"Mom told you something, didn't she?" Solenne said. "About how to fight them."

"She did." Hunter stood slowly. His legs steadied. The chevrons pulsed stronger, responding to his determination. "But it's going to cost me everything."

"No." Solenne grabbed his arm. "Dad, you just found me. We just, we haven't even talked yet. About your life, my life, Mom's sacrifice. I haven't told you about growing up. About how I searched for you across every timeline. About how many times I almost gave up but didn't because I knew you were out there somewhere. You can't just—"

"I have to." Hunter knelt again, eye level with his daughter. "Solenne, listen. Your mother gave up everything to save you. To buy me time to become strong enough to end this. I'm not going to waste her sacrifice by choosing the safe path."

"What if you die?"

"Then I die knowing I saved my daughter." Hunter touched her face gently. "In any timeline, that's a good death."

Tears streamed down Solenne's face. "I've been alone for so long. I can't lose you too. Not when I just got you back."

Hunter pulled her into his arms. She buried her face against his scaled chest, sobbing. He held his daughter. This brave, fierce, determined girl who'd crossed timelines to save him, and let himself feel it. The love. The grief. The impossible joy of finally holding her.

"You won't lose me," he whispered into her hair. "Not really. Whatever happens, I'll always be part of you. That's what it means to be a fixed point. I exist in all moments. Past, present, future. I'll always be there, Solenne. In every memory. Every choice. Every timeline where you need me."

She pulled back, wiping her eyes. "Promise?"

"I promise." He met her green eyes. "I'll fix this. I'll bring you guys home, even if it means—"

The building shook violently. Through the windows, shadow figures materialized, dozens of them. Then hundreds. An army of Ouroboros, drawn by the tablet's activation like sharks to blood.

Hugo appeared from the shadows. "They come, come. Many, many. Too many, many."

Hunter stood, helping Sloan to her feet. He looked at the old man. "Get her out of here."

"Dad—"

"No arguments." Hunter's voice held the machines. "Hugo, there's an exit. I saw it in the visions. A portal to somewhere safe."

"Yes, yes. Already open, open." Hugo gestured toward a doorway that pulsed with gold light.

"Take her through. Keep her safe until this is over."

Solenne grabbed his arm. "What if it's not over? What if you—"

"Then you survive." Hunter squeezed her hand. "You survive and you live. You find someone who loves you. You have children. You tell them about your father who existed in all timelines at once, who loved you so much he fought an army to keep you safe. Can you do that?"

Solenne nodded, tears streaming. "What about mom?"

"She'll be right by your side." Hunter kissed her forehead. "Go. Now."

Hugo took Solenne's hand. She clutched the Jar, Evelyne's face pressed against the crystal watching her daughter leave.

I love you, baby, Evelyne's voice echoed in Hunter's mind. *So much.*

I know, Mom. Solenne looked back one last time at Hunter. "Dad, thank you. For everything. For remembering. For fighting. For—"

"Go!" Hunter pushed her toward Hugo.

The old man pulled Solenne through the golden doorway. It sealed behind them with a sound like thunder, and they were gone. Hunter stood alone in the strange corridor. The building shook again. Plaster rained from the ceiling. Outside, the Ouroboros army pressed closer. Hundreds of them. Maybe thousands. Shadow figures with glowing eyes, drawn by the tablet's power.

Hunter walked toward the door. The chevrons blazed purple across his entire body. Scales covering every inch of skin, pulsing with each heartbeat. He could feel the tablet integrated into his palm, holding him together across infinite realities.

He pushed open the door and stepped onto the street. The Ouroboros surrounded the building. An army of shadow, filling the street, climbing walls, hovering in the air. Their eyes glowed in the growing darkness. Hundreds of them. All focused on him.

"You have the tablet," one said. Its voice layered with harmonics. "Surrender it. Become one of us. Or we erase you from every timeline."

Hunter raised his hand, the tablet blazing with light embedded in his palm. "I have a counteroffer."

"You're in no position to negotiate."

"Who's negotiating?" Hunter felt power surge through him. Every version of himself across every timeline focused on this single moment. "I'm using the tablet not to stabilize myself, but to weaponize the Rippling. I'm going to turn your own timeline manipulation against you."

The Ouroboros laughed. A chorus of haunting coos that made the air vibrate.

"Imbecilic. That would destroy you too."

"I know." Hunter smiled grimly. "But I'm willing to die for the people I love. What would you die for?"

Silence.

"That's what I thought." Hunter slammed his palm into the ground. "You gave up your soul to become eternal. Let me show you what you lost."

Reality fractured.

Pain exploded through Hunter's skull. The chevrons burned like brands pressed into flesh. He felt his consciousness spreading and tearing, ripping across infinite timelines. Each piece of himself fragmenting, scattering, attacking from every angle at once.

In one timeline, he found the Ouroboros command structure, a crystalline web connecting all of them across realities. He grabbed it with mental hands and squeezed. The web shattered.

"No! That's impossible."

In another timeline, he severed their connection to the Dall. The source of their power. The ancient structure that sustained them across millennia. He watched it crumble and felt them screaming as their anchor dissolved.

"Stop! You're destroying everything."

In a third timeline, he found the original Ouroboros. The first one. The creature that had sacrificed its humanity thousands of years ago to become eternal. It looked at him with ancient eyes, lifetimes of regret.

"You don't understand what you're doing, it whispered. If we fall, the timelines collapse.

Everything ends."

"Who's the imbecile, now?" Hunter said. "They will live in a universe without you."

He destroyed the original Ouroboros, The Sovereign. Felt it dissolve across every timeline, taking its descendants with it.

The shadow figures on the street screamed, a sound that shattered windows, cracked pavement, made the air itself vibrate with agony. They clawed at their faces, their chests, trying to hold themselves together as Hunter tore through their existence timeline by timeline. But the cost.

Hunter felt himself coming apart. His consciousness scattered too thin across infinite realities. He was dying in one timeline, being born in another, killing the Time Recorder again, standing in Williams' interrogation room, holding Ember as a baby, watching Tara die, marrying Evelyne, meeting Solenne for the first time. All at once. All simultaneously. All him.

His bones felt like they were being pulled apart and stitched back together. The chevrons across his body cracked, blazing white-hot, burning through flesh. Blood poured from his nose, his ears, black, red, black again. The smell of ozone mixed with burnt copper, so strong he could taste it.

In the physical timeline, he collapsed. His hands clawed at the pavement. The shadow figures continued dissolving around him, but Hunter couldn't hold on much longer. He was fracturing. Scattering. Becoming nothing.

"Dad!" Solenne's voice was distant. From somewhere across timelines.

"Hold on! Just hold on!"

But he couldn't. He was everywhere and nowhere. Every version of himself screaming as consciousness fragmented beyond recovery. The tablet in his palm pulsed wildly, trying to hold him together, but it wasn't enough.

He'd destroyed the Ouroboros. But he'd destroyed himself too.

Hunter opened his eyes, one last time. The street was empty. No shadow figures. No army. Just pavement and broken glass and the smell of something burning. He had won. And now he was going to die.

Solenne, he thought across timelines. "I'm sorry. I tried to stay. I tried"

Then something happened. A pulse of light from the tablet. Not destructive but stitching him together. It spread through Hunter's body, gathering the scattered pieces of his consciousness, pulling them back together. Not human anymore. Not Ouroboros either. Something new. Something that existed in all timelines but remained whole.

A true fixed point. The chevrons across his body stopped burning. They pulsed once, bright purple, then faded to a soft glow. The blood stopped flowing. The pain receded. Hunter rose. His hands were steady. The scales remained, but they felt different now. Not alien. Part of him. Integrated.

He walked, testing his balance. Everything ached, but he was whole. Transformed, but whole. Golden light exploded behind him. Solenne and Hugo emerged from the portal. His daughter ran to him, tears streaming, and crashed into his arms.

"You did it!" she sobbed. "You actually did it! They're gone. All of them. Across every timeline. I felt it. The Rippling stopped. Everything stabilized."

Hunter held her tight, feeling more human than he had since this all began. "It worked?"

"It worked." Solenne pulled back, studying his face. The scales. The glowing chevrons. "But Dad, you look... different."

"I am different." Hunter looked at his hands. Not quite human. Not quite Ouroboros. Something in between. "I'm a fixed point that chose to remain. To stay human even when it should have been impossible."

Solenne smiled through her tears. "Mom said you would. She said love was stronger than any cosmic force."

"She usually is." Hunter looked down at the Jar in Solenne's arms. Inside, Evelyne pressed her hand against the crystal. He placed his palm against it from outside.

You saved us, he thought to her. All of us.

No, Evelyne's voice whispered in his mind. We saved each other. That's what family does. Thunder rolled one last time. But the sky was clearing. The Rippling had stopped. The timelines stabilized. Hunter had weaponized the collapse, destroyed the Ouroboros, and survived by refusing to become the monster they wanted.

The watch in his pocket stopped pulsing. Three-thirty-three faded. Time moved forward again, linear and clean.

"What now?" Solenne asked.

Hunter looked at his daughter. At the Jar containing his wife from another timeline. At Hugo standing nearby, those clothespin lenses reflecting the streetlights.

"Now we get your mother out of that prison," he said. "Then we figure out what comes next. Together."

Solenne's smile widened. "All three of us?"

"All three of us." Hunter pulled her close. "We're a family, Solenne. Across every timeline. In every possibility. And I'm never letting you go again."

Behind them, the empty street remained silent. No Ouroboros. No threats. Just a father and daughter and the promise of a future they would build together. One choice, one moment, one timeline at a time.

The storm had passed. And for the first time since Tara died, since everything went wrong, since he became something more than human, Hunter felt hope.

Somewhere else. Somewhen else.

The Sovereign's static whisper entered Hunter's brain from across timelines, penetrating the barrier he thought he'd built, there are infinite possibilities. *You cannot escape us. You never could.*

Hunter staggered, clutching his head. The voice faded, but the threat remained.

In a chamber that existed outside linear time, Arlowe turned the

Time Recorder's scale with the tip of a scalpel. She had found it glowing faintly in the chamber shortly after Hunter vanished into the void, a piece of the creature he'd destroyed was still transmitting.

"You see? It flickered again." She bent closer, fascinated and disturbed. "It keeps transmitting no matter what I do to it."

Madam Synod kneaded her chin, a concerned look etched on her ancient face. "Burning does nothing. Freezing does nothing. Even the Dall's alloy seems powerless against it." She turned to stare at the scale, watching it pulse with impossible light. "We need him. Hunter Persefoni. I don't think there's any other way."

"But he destroyed the Ouroboros," Arlowe said. "He thinks it's over."

"Oh, child." Madam Synod's smile was cold. "It's never over. The Ouroboros were merely soldiers. The Sovereign—" She gestured to the pulsing scale. "That's the general. And it's been waiting for Hunter to become strong enough to be worth taking."

The scale pulsed brighter, and somewhere across infinite timelines, Hunter felt the first stirring of something ancient turning its attention toward him.

The fight had only just begun.

part fifteen
the fall

Hunter stood in his apartment, the Jar pulsing in Solenne's hands. Through the crystal, Evelyne's face pressed against the barrier, watching them. His wife from another timeline. His wife was also Tara. The woman he'd loved across infinite realities.

"The tablet will free her," Solenne said, voice convinced, even hopeful. "Hugo said if we channel its power through the Jar, we can break the prison. But we need—"

Thunder cracked inside Hunter's skull. Not the familiar rolling thunder of timeline bleeding. This was different. Sharper and lethal. The Sovereign's static whisper penetrated his mind like needles.

There are infinite possibilities. You cannot escape us. You never could.

"Dad?" Solenne stepped back, clutching the sphere tighter. "What's wrong?"

Hunter staggered, gripping the kitchen counter. The chevrons across his body blazed purple, responding to the threat. Through the window, he saw reality itself beginning to fracture. The building across the street flickered between brick and something crystalline, the street below shifting between asphalt and liquid darkness.

"They're here."

"Who's here?"

"The ones who made the Ouroboros." Hunter grabbed her shoulders. The scales on his hands felt rough against her jacket. "Listen to me. The tablet showed me everything. Evelyne isn't just Evelyne. She's—"

"I know." Tears streamed down Solenne's face. "She's Mom. I've always known. She told me before she went into the Jar. She said when you were ready, when you'd transformed enough, you'd remember."

Hunter pulled his daughter close, feeling her heartbeat against his scaled chest. "And you. Those green eyes. I should have known the moment I saw you at the train station."

"I'm Ember," she whispered. "I grew up across the timelines while you were becoming this. Hugo kept me safe. Taught me how to move between realities. How to find you." Her voice broke. "I've been searching for you my whole life, Dad. Every timeline. Every possibility. I never gave up."

The apartment windows shattered. Not from impact. From an evil presence. Reality itself fractured as The Sovereign manifested, not fully, but enough. A shape of living darkness that wore the outline of something that had once been human, millennia ago, before it chose eternity over love. Its voice came from everywhere and nowhere.

"Wars are never won on battlefields, Hunter Persefoni. They are won in the mouths of those who speak. The greatest weapon ever forged wasn't steel or gunpowder. It was language. Long ago, your kind learned to build towers together. So someone tore the tower down and scattered your tongues. We need not enslave you. You do it to each other with every word. Every nation, every tribe, every god you worship, language made them all. We do not conquer. We translate your ruin."

The darkness surged closer, swallowing the apartment's light. Hunter could feel it probing his mind, searching for weaknesses, for the connections that made him vulnerable.

"And you, you are the greatest threat to our Dominion. Not because you're powerful. But because you still feel. Because the transformation didn't take your humanity. You refuse to let them go."

Hunter pushed Solenne behind him.

The Sovereign's laughter was like static electricity across his skin.

"Love is the leash we use to control you. The chain that makes you predictable, watch."

The darkness reached for Solenne. She gasped as invisible fingers closed around her throat. The Jar slipped from her hands, hitting the floor with a sound like breaking glass. Inside, Evelyne screamed silently, pressing her hands against the crystal.

"Let her go!" Hunter lunged forward, but The Sovereign's power held him frozen.

"You see? Love makes you weak. Makes you desperate. Makes you—"

"—sacrifice," Hunter finished.

The word unlocked something inside him. A clarity that cut through The Sovereign's manipulation like a blade through shadow. He understood now what Evelyne had known when she activated the Jar. What Williams would realize when he faced the aliens. What had driven Hugo across timelines to guide him.

Love wasn't the weakness. Love was the weapon they could never understand. Hunter stopped fighting The Sovereign's hold. Instead, he reached inward, to where the tablet was embedded in his palm, pulsing with power that connected him to every timeline at once.

"Solenne," he said. "Remember what Evelyne taught you. The portal sequence."

The darkness released her. She collapsed, gasping, clutching her throat. "No. Not without you. We free Mom together. That was the plan."

"Plans change." Hunter raised his palm. Golden light erupted from the tablet, and a doorway materialized behind Solenne, pure white, radiating warmth and safety. The escape route. "The Sovereign wants me. Let them have me."

"Dad, NO!" Solenne grabbed his arm, trying to pull him toward the portal.

Hunter pried her fingers loose and mouthed I love you. The Sovereign's darkness was closing in, seconds away from consuming them both. "It's okay to let go."

"I can't!" Solenne's voice broke into a sob. "Growing up knowing my father existed somewhere but couldn't remember me? Please, Dad, PLEASE—"

Hunter cupped her face with his scaled hands. Looked into those green eyes, his eyes, passed down through genetics and love and cosmic impossibility.

"You never lost me, baby. I was scattered across timelines, but I was always there. Watching. Protecting when I could. And I'll be there again." His voice cracked. "But right now, you need to LIVE. You need to free your mother. You need to be the light that survives."

He shoved her through the portal. She fought, screaming, clawing at the golden doorway's edges as it began to close. Her hand stretched toward him, fingers splayed, desperate.

"DAD! DAD! Don't leave me."

The last thing Hunter saw was her face. Seventeen-year-old Solenne's face with six-year-old Ember's expression of pure devastation, betrayal twisted in anguish, reaching for him as the light consumed her.

The portal was sealed with a sound like thunder. Then silence. Hunter stood alone in his shattered apartment, The Sovereign's darkness pressing closer. Glass crunched under his feet. Wind howled through the broken windows. Eighteen floors below, the city spread before him like the past. Like the old him.

The Sovereign's grimace smile rose. "You think sacrifice will save her? We are eternal. We will find her. We will find them all. And when we do, we'll make you watch as we corrupt everything you love."

"Infinite possibilities." Hunter walked toward the window. His mind raced through options, calculating possibilities the way the tablet had taught him to see reality, as layers of choice and consequence stacked infinitely high. "Isn't that what you said?"

Fight The Sovereign here, Solenne dies when the battle collapses this section of the building. Hundreds of civilians die. The Jar shatters with Evelyne inside. Run, they'd never stop hunting. Solenne would spend her life fleeing. Evelyne would rot in crystal prison forever. Surrender and become their weapon. Watch himself destroy everyone he loves, conscious but powerless to stop it. Or jump. Let the tablet's power scatter him across timelines like a corrupted code. Let his dissolution fuel Solenne's escape and Evelyne's freedom. Become the sacrifice that breaks their control.

I've died before, Hunter thought. On that road where Tara and Ember died. In the Dall when I killed the Time Recorder. In a thousand timelines where different versions of me made different choices. What's one more death if it means they live.

He thought about Tara's last words before the crash: "I love you. No matter what happens next, remember I love you."

He thought about Ember's laugh, the real Ember. Six years old, chasing butterflies in Central Park before everything went wrong. He thought about Evelyne walking into that conference room, activating the Jar, choosing imprisonment to buy him time. He thought about Solenne, his daughter across timelines, who'd never given up on him. I love you all, Hunter thought. Across every reality. In every possibility, forever.

The Sovereign screamed, a sound that shattered the remaining windows, that made the building shake, that rippled across six city blocks. "What are you—"

One second.

Hunter jumped. The wind tore at him immediately. His suit jacket flapped like broken wings. Glass fragments from the shattered window tumbled alongside him, catching streetlight, glittering like stars. Eighteen floors, 180 feet. He'd calculated it once in another life. It takes roughly 3.5 seconds to fall that far. He had 3.5 seconds to say goodbye to being human.

He could see his reflection in the building's windows as he fell past them. Each reflection showed a different version. Human Hunter in one, scaled Hunter in another, dissolved Hunter in a third, dead Hunter in a fourth, alive Hunter in a fifth. All of them falling simultaneously, all of them real, all of them him.

Two seconds.

The chevrons across his body blazed purple, trying to save him. The tablet in his palm pulsed frantically, calculating survival possibilities across infinite timelines, finding none that didn't involve compromise. His consciousness began fragmenting, scattering like light through a prism, splitting into every version of himself that had ever existed.

He saw Solenne's face in the portal—Ember's face—green eyes wide with horror and love and desperation. He saw Evelyne through the Jar crystal, pressing her hands against the barrier, knowing what he was about to do. He saw Tara smiling on their wedding day, saying "I do" like it was the easiest promise in the world.

Three seconds.

The city rushed up to meet him. Concrete and steel and the promise of transformation. He could hear The Sovereign pursuing, dark tendrils reaching through the falling space, trying to claim him before impact, trying to catch him and bend him and break him into the weapon they needed.

But Hunter had one advantage they didn't anticipate. He wasn't afraid to die. Because he'd already died. On that road. In the Dall. In a thousand timelines. Death was just another transformation. Another way of loving so hard it transcended flesh and bone and time itself.

Four seconds.

The pavement.

Hunter closed his eyes. Heard Solenne scream across dimensions. "DAD!"

Heard Evelyne whispering from inside the Jar. *I've got you, my love. I've always got you.*

Heard the tablet's final pulse surge through his body. And then nothing. Everything. The space between impact.

part sixteen
the righteous

11:49 p.m.

"Are you sure about the gold mesh?" John Williams touched the lining of his baseball cap as they drove down the last few blocks toward Hunter Persefoni's address.

Eli Spencer checked his weapon for the third time, fingers moving with practiced efficiency. "I had a dream about it last night. Divine guidance or PTSD, hell if I know. But it'll block their signal. Stop them from freezing us like last time."

"The last time we died," John said flatly, eyes fixed on the building ahead.

"The last time we died," Eli confirmed. "And got resurrected by men in black who told us to protect Hunter Persefoni at all costs." He slammed the magazine back into place. "You ever think about how insane that sounds?"

John almost smiled. "Every goddamn day."

They fell silent, each lost in thoughts too dark to voice. John's hands tightened on the wheel. Somewhere up there, in that building looming against the night sky, Hunter was in danger. He could feel it, that same pull he'd felt on the road where they first encountered the aliens. The weight of divine purpose pressing down on his shoulders like armor forged from starlight.

You are the armor of all things light, the voice in his dream had said. *Remember who you are.*

But who was he? A cop who'd died and been resurrected? A warrior who'd fought aliens across lifetimes he couldn't remember. A man who saw his children's spiritual essence being consumed by reptilian creatures every time he closed his eyes.

All of it. None of it. Something in between.

"You really think we can trust him?" Eli asked quietly. "Hunter?"

John stared at the building. "The voice said protect him. Same voice that brought us back from death. What else do you need?"

"Even if he's a monster? Even if those scales we saw mean he's becoming one of them?"

"He's not one of them." John's jaw clenched. "I've fought these things before. I don't know how I know that, but I do. Different life. Different universe. Feels like remembering a dream that belonged to someone else. And I can tell you this, the real monsters don't sacrifice themselves. They don't love. They don't bleed. Hunter does all three."

Eli nodded slowly. "Okay. Then we—" He stopped.

They'd rounded the corner, and the crowd was already forming.

People everywhere. Pointing up. Screaming. Cell phones raised, recording. John followed their collective gaze to the eighteenth floor where a window had shattered, curtain whipping violently in the wind.

"Jesus Christ," Eli breathed.

Then they saw him.

Hunter.

Falling.

Body limp, arms spread like he was embracing the sky. Purple light blazing across every inch of visible skin. Those chevrons they'd seen in the interrogation room, now covering him completely. He looked less like a man and more like a falling star.

"He jumped," someone in the crowd said.

"Call 911!" another screamed.

"Oh my God, oh my God—"

"No." John was already moving, Eli right behind him. "He was pushed."

They reached the impact site seconds after Hunter hit.

The sound, John would never forget that sound. Like thunder compressed into a single moment. Like the universe itself had cracked open and spilled out something it wasn't meant to contain.

He pushed through the crowd, badge already out. "Move! Federal investigation! Everyone back—"

Then he saw it.

Hunter Persefoni lay twisted on the concrete, limbs at impossible angles. Blood pooled around him, spreading like dark water. But it kept shifting colors, black, then red, then black again, then something purple that glowed faintly, as if his body couldn't decide which timeline to die in.

Glass fragments adorned him like diamonds. His suit was shredded. And the scales, those purple scales covered every visible inch of skin, pulsing weakly like dying stars.

John's breath caught.

He'd seen a lot of death in his career. Seen bodies mangled in car crashes, shootings, domestic violence. Seen what humanity did to itself when darkness won. Seen children who'd been hurt in ways that made him question God's existence.

But this, this was different.

Hunter shouldn't be alive. The fall alone would have liquefied his internal organs. The impact should have turned him into meat and bone fragments. No one survived eighteen floors.

And yet—

"He has a pulse," a woman said.

John spun. A woman in hospital scrubs knelt beside Hunter's body, fingers pressed to his neck. Her badge read Dr. Miriam Chen, Mount Sinai ER.

"That's impossible," Eli said. "Nobody survives that fall."

"His pulse is there." Dr. Chen's voice was steady, professional. "Faint. Irregular. But there. Core temperature is stable somehow. I don't understand it, but he's fighting to stay alive."

John knelt beside Hunter's broken form. Up close, he could see the scales shifting, responding to breath, to heartbeat, to something beyond human physiology. Reality seemed to bend around him, like he existed in multiple places at once.

This is what The Sovereign fears, John thought. Not because he's powerful. Because he refuses to give up. Because he still loves.

"We need to stabilize him," Dr. Chen said. "But I can't move him. Not with these injuries. One wrong shift and—"

"He'll die," John finished.

"Yes."

Eli grabbed John's arm. "Williams. Look."

John followed his gaze up. On the eighteenth floor, in the broken window, a shape moved. Not human. Not quite. Living darkness that watched them with interest.

The ones who did this, John thought. His hand moved to his weapon.

"Not yet," Eli whispered, reading his intention. "Too many civilians. If we start shooting now."

"I know."

The shape withdrew, sliding back into the apartment like smoke.

"Ambulance incoming," someone in the crowd called out. "I can hear sirens!"

But John's instincts screamed wrong. The sound was off. Too close. Like it had been waiting around the corner rather than responding to a call.

An ambulance screeched into view, moving too fast, taking the corner recklessly. It skidded to a stop in front of them, and two paramedics rushed out.

One was small, elderly, wearing clothespins in place of proper medical equipment. The other was a woman in her twenties with green eyes that seemed to glow in the streetlight.

John's breath caught again.

He knew those eyes.

Not from this lifetime. From somewhere else. Some other reality where everything had gone differently. Where those green eyes had looked up at him and called him

Uncle John? Will you push me on the swing?

No. That was impossible. That was a memory that didn't exist, couldn't exist, belonged to a dream or another life, but he knew better.

"We'll take it from here," the small paramedic said in a strange stutter. "He good, good. We fix, fix."

Eli stepped forward. "Who are you? What's your unit number? This isn't protocol."

But the girl was already kneeling beside Hunter, and John saw her face clearly for the first time.

Tears streamed down her cheeks. Her hands shook as she checked Hunter's vitals. She looked at his broken body with an expression John had seen a thousand times in his career.

The way a daughter looks at her dying father.

"He's still here," she whispered, more to herself than anyone. "He's still fighting."

"Miss," John said gently. "What's your name?"

She looked up. For just a moment, their eyes met, and John saw everything. Timelines bleeding together, alternate realities where he'd known this girl, where they'd been family, where he'd been the uncle who taught her to ride a bike and scared away bullies and walked her down the aisle.

None of it real. All of it true.

"We'll take care of him," she said, voice thick with heartbreak. "I promise. He won't die. Not today."

"How can you be sure?"

"Because he's my—" She stopped. Looked at the small paramedic, who shook his head slightly. "Because that's what we do. We save people."

They loaded Hunter onto a stretcher with impossible gentleness, as if moving something precious and irreplaceable. The girl climbed into the back of the ambulance, never taking her eyes off him.

"Wait," John called out. "Where are you taking him?"

But the ambulance was already pulling away, sirens blaring.

Eli grabbed John's arm. "That wasn't real. That ambulance, those paramedics. None of that was protocol. We should've stopped them. We should've—"

"Let them go."

"What?"

John watched the ambulance disappear around a corner. "She was crying, Eli. The girl. She looked at Hunter's body and she was crying." He turned to face his partner. "The aliens don't cry. They don't feel. They consume. They corrupt. They enslave. But they don't weep for the dying."

"So what does that mean?"

"It means Hunter isn't just some billionaire suspect. He's someone's father. Someone's husband. Someone worth dying for." John looked at the blood on the pavement, still shifting colors, still refusing to settle into one timeline. "Which means he's someone worth killing aliens over."

A chill ran down John's spine.

He felt it before he saw it, the temperature drop, the sudden absence of sound, the world beginning to slow.

"Eli."

John saw it happen in slow motion.

The woman nearest him stopped mid-word. Her mouth hung open, frozen on a syllable. A businessman's coffee cup tilted, liquid suspended in mid-pour, defying gravity like physics had forgotten how to work.

Then the cars. One by one, vehicles froze mid-motion. Traffic lights stopped cycling. A bird overhead, wings spread, hung motionless like a taxidermy display.

The dog three blocks away, John could still see it clearly, leg raised against a hydrant, stream of piss frozen in a golden arc that shouldn't be physically possible.

Everything and everyone just stopped.

Except John could still move. Still breathe. And the gold mesh lining his cap hummed against his skull, vibrating with energy.

"Eli," John whispered. "Don't. Move."

But Eli was staring at his own hand. He'd been reaching for his weapon, and his fingers had stopped halfway. frozen by whatever force was taking hold. Only his eyes moved, terrified, looking at John for answers he didn't have.

Then the force released him.

Eli gasped, stumbling forward. "What the fuck."

"The mesh works," John said. "But barely. Whatever they're doing, it almost got you."

That's when they appeared.

Two women walking through the frozen crowd. Beautiful. Blonde. Identical. They moved with impossible grace, as if gravity affected them differently. Their eyes shifted colors, blue, gray, green, then something reptilian underneath the glamour.

The Smith sisters. The Ouroboros.

John had dreamed about these women. Watched them transform into white serpents with skin that sparkled like diamonds. Watched them consume children's spiritual essence like vampires feeding on light. Watched them in a hundred timelines, in a thousand nightmares, in memories that belonged to lives he'd never lived.

They stopped ten feet away, studying John and Eli with venomous interest.

"Interesting," one of them said with a static echo. "The mesh protects your thoughts. Clever. Desperate. But clever. Tell me, Mr. Williams, where did you acquire such trinkets?"

"A dream told me," John said calmly. "From voices that brought me back from death."

The woman's smile widened. "Ah. So you've met the others. The interferers. The ones who insist humanity has potential." She laughed, a sound like breaking glass. "We've been managing this species for millennia. Believe me when I say, humanity peaked centuries ago. Now you're just livestock with delusions of grandeur."

"Where's the third one?" John said quietly.

Eli's eyes went wide. "What?"

"They always travel in threes. Aliens, demons, whatever the fuck they are. They hunt in packs." John's hand moved closer to his weapon. "Two in front. One behind. Classic flanking maneuver. Where is she?"

A voice answered from near Hunter's blood pool, feminine and ice cold. A slither rose. "Right here, Mr. Williams. Observing. Always observing."

John spun. A third blonde woman stood where Hunter had fallen, one perfect hand hovering over the blood, sensing something, reading it, extracting information from the shifting colors.

"Such power," she murmured. "Wasted on sentiment. Squandered on love. If we could harness just a fraction of what he's become—" She looked up, eyes blazing. "We want him. Hand over the trail. Tell us where your little ambulance friends took him. Or your families are next."

"You already tried that speech," John said. "On the road. Right before you killed us."

The woman's smile didn't reach her eyes. "And yet here you stand. Curious, isn't it? Death doesn't seem to hold you. Perhaps you're more like us than you realize. Perhaps you've already transcended humanity without knowing it."

"We're nothing like you."

"No?" The woman gestured to the frozen crowd with disdain. "They're sheep, Mr. Williams. You're shepherds. We're shepherds. The only difference is scale."

Before John could respond, Eli stepped forward, voice sharp. "We're not stupid, lady. You threatened our families. This is only going one way ?"

The alien tilted her head, curious.

"I learned that evil doesn't negotiate. It enslaves, it consumes." Eli's weapon came up smooth, barrel aimed center mass on the leader. "So here's our offer, you leave this planet. All of you. Every timeline. Or we hunt you down one by one until there's nothing left but ash."

John felt pride surge through him. "That's my partner."

The leader's smile vanished. Her face shifted, just for a moment, revealing something reptilian underneath. White scales. Eyes too large. A mouth that snapped like a snake's.

"Fool," she hissed. "You have no idea what you're challenging. We are eternal. We are—"

"Mortal," John interrupted. He'd seen it in his dreams. Seen their weakness. Seen how to kill them. "You die just like everything else. You just convinced yourselves otherwise."

The leader's eyes blazed. "Kill them."

The two blonde women near Eli moved with inhuman speed, but John was faster.

He'd seen this moment a thousand times in dreams he couldn't fully remember. Practiced it across lifetimes that belonged to someone else. His weapon came up smooth and sure, muscle memory from battles he'd never fought, and he fired.

Not at the drones.

At the leader.

The bullet struck her chest center mass.

For a split second, nothing happened.

Then she screamed.

Not a human scream. A frequency that shattered already-broken windows, cracked pavement, made John's teeth ache and Eli drop to one knee. The two drones echoed the sound. Three voices harmonizing into a weapon that should have liquefied their internal organs.

But the gold mesh held.

John felt it vibrating against his skull, absorbing the sonic attack, protecting his mind from the frequency that would have turned his brain into soup.

He emptied his clip into the leader.

Each shot made her scream louder. Her body fractured like porcelain, cracks spreading across that perfect skin. Light poured from the wounds, not blood but pure energy, like she was a vessel containing something that didn't belong in this dimension.

"They're dying!" Eli shouted over the noise, his own weapon raised. "They're actually fucking dying!"

The leader collapsed.

The moment she hit the pavement, her body exploded into fine white dust. The two drones followed immediately. Their screams cutting off as they disintegrated, three alien entities reduced to ash in seconds.

John stood over the pile of white dust, weapon still smoking, chest heaving.

Time snapped back.

The world lurched into motion. The crowd surged forward, confused, talking over each other. The businessman's coffee finished pouring. The dog finished pissing. The bird flew away.

No one remembered freezing. No one saw the aliens dissolve. To them, there had just been a loud noise, a car backfiring, maybe, and now two federal agents stood in the street looking shaken.

"Are you hit?" John grabbed Eli's shoulder.

"No." Eli stared at the ash pile. "We killed them. We actually killed them."

"Yeah."

"What if there are more?"

"There are definitely more." John holstered his weapon, hands shaking slightly from adrenaline. "Which means this was just the opening move. They'll come after us now. After Hunter. After everyone who knows the truth."

Eli pulled the victory bottle from his jacket, the one he'd brought for when they closed big cases. "Then we'd better get ready for war."

"Not war," John corrected. He looked up at the eighteenth floor, at the broken window, at the darkness that still lurked somewhere inside. "Hunt. We're not soldiers anymore, Eli. We're hunters. And it's time to start taking down monsters."

The crowd pressed closer, asking questions. Police were arriving, actual police this time, responding to reports of a jumper. John and Eli would have to give statements. Explain what they were doing here. Spin a story that wouldn't get them locked up.

But as John looked at the ash pile, already scattering in the wind, already disappearing like the aliens had never existed, he felt something settle inside him.

Purpose.

For years he'd been investigating crimes after they happened. Cleaning up messes. Documenting evil without preventing it.

Not anymore.

Now he was going to war. Against an enemy that had enslaved humanity for millennia. Against creatures that corrupted love and consumed souls and pretended to be divine.

And somewhere, in an ambulance that wasn't really an ambulance, with paramedics who weren't really paramedics, Hunter Persefoni was being taken somewhere safe.

Protect him, the voice had said.

Well. John had protected him from three Ouroboros. Now it was

Hunter's turn to heal. To transform. To become whatever weapon the universe needed.

And when Hunter was ready, when he came back from whatever journey he was on, John Williams would be there. Ready to fight alongside him. Ready to burn the Ouroboros empire to ash.

The armor of all things light, he thought, remembering the dream. That's who I am.

He just hoped it would be enough.

part seventeen
space between

11:52 p.m.

The space between moments, Hunter opened his eyes to white. Not hospital white. Not death white. Something older. Primordial. The color before color existed. Before light knew how to separate from darkness. And before the universe remembered it was supposed to have physics.

He was standing, or floating, he couldn't tell which, in a space that had no up or down. No walls. No ceiling. Just endless white that somehow felt... warm and alive. Breathing with a rhythm he could almost feel against his skin.

When he looked at his hands, they flickered. Solid one moment, scales and all. And transparent the next, revealing nothing underneath, or everything, or the infinite possibilities between existence and void.

He could see through his fingers timelines stacked like windows. In one, he was still falling. In another, he'd never jumped. In a third, he'd died on impact. In a fourth, he was already healing. All of them real. All of them happening simultaneously.

"Are you ready?"

Hunter turned. Hugo sat legs akimbo on nothing, hovering at eye level. Behind him, darkness churned. Not empty darkness, but darkness full of movement. Full of screaming. Hunter could see shapes in there. Faces pressing against some invisible membrane. The Rippling. The end of all timelines condensed into a hungry void that wanted to consume everything.

"Where am I?" Hunter's voice echoed strangely, as if speaking from multiple throats.

"Between." Hugo's voice carried harmonics that shouldn't exist. "Between breath and death. Between human and eternal. Between all the choices you've made and all the ones you'll never make. Your body is dying on a sidewalk in New York. Your daughter is fighting the Rippling outside an ambulance. Your wife is trapped in crystal, waiting for rescue. You exist in all these moments simultaneously because you're a fixed point. The question is, which moment will you choose?"

Hunter's chest tightened, or would have, if he still had a chest in the traditional sense. "Am I dead?"

"Not yet. But your body is dying. Multiple organ failure. Spinal fracture. Skull fracture. Internal bleeding. In any normal timeline, you'd have minutes at most." Hugo gestured to the churning darkness. "But you're not in a normal timeline anymore. You're in the space where timelines are born. Where possibilities become reality. Where choice matters more than physics."

Hunter looked at his flickering hands. At the scales that pulsed with faint purple light. At everything he'd become. "What happens if I choose wrong?"

"There is no wrong choice. Only consequences." Hugo stood, and suddenly he wasn't small anymore. He grew, expanded, became something vast and ancient. A being that existed across multiple dimensions, wearing Hugo's form the way Hunter wore his scaled skin. "The tablet brought you here to decide. Become fully fixed, lose your humanity, exist forever trapped in all moments at once, eternal but empty. You'll be conscious in every timeline simultaneously, unable to die, unable to truly live. Watching everyone you love age and die in infinite variations while you remain unchanged."

"That sounds like hell."

"Yes." Hugo's smile was infinitely sad. "Or dissolve. Scatter your consciousness across infinite timelines until there's nothing left of who you were. No memories. No identity. Just energy distributed so thin you cease to be Hunter Persefoni and become… nothing. Everything. The light between moments that no one remembers."

Hunter closed his eyes. Both options sounded like death. "Those are my only choices?"

"No." Hugo's voice dropped to a whisper. "Infinite possibilities. The Ouroboros never anticipated because they stopped understanding love millennia ago. One that requires you to see the truth about who you are. About whom they are. About what Evelyne and Solenne really mean."

The void shifted.

Hunter saw Evelyne inside the Jar, pressing her hands against crystal. But as he watched, her face changed. Became Tara. Brown hair shifted to lighter. Blue eyes deepened to brown. The woman he'd married. The woman he'd lost on that road.

"Evelyne is Tara reincarnated," Hugo said. "Same soul. Different timeline. The tablet brought her back after the crash. Gave her memories of both lives. She remembers loving you as Tara. Remembers dying in that accident. And she remembers loving you again as Evelyne, meeting you in this timeline, trying to save you from the Ouroboros."

Hunter's throat tightened. "She knew? The whole time?"

"Yes. That's why she sacrificed herself. Not just to buy you time. But because she'd already lost you once. She wasn't going to lose you again. Even if it meant trapping herself in crystal for eternity."

The void shifted again. Hunter saw Solenne, his daughter, seventeen years old, fierce and determined. But superimposed over her. He saw six-year-old Ember in the back seat of the car, screaming as the accident unfolded.

"And Solenne?" Hunter whispered, though he already knew.

"She's Ember," Hugo confirmed. "The tablet preserved her soul when the crash happened. Placed her in another timeline. Aged her across realities while you transformed. She grew up knowing her father existed somewhere but couldn't remember her. Spent her entire life searching for you. Training with me. Learning to move between timelines. Never giving up hope."

Hunter felt his consciousness fracturing under the weight of revelation. "I have a family. Across timelines. Tara and Ember, they're still with me. They never left."

"No. They transformed. Became Evelyne and Solenne. Love doesn't die, Hunter. It just changes shape."

Thunder rolled through the void.

Not natural thunder. The Rippling. Growing closer. Consuming reality piece by piece. Hunter could hear screaming from inside the darkness. Souls being torn apart. Timelines collapsing. The universe forgetting how to hold itself together.

"Solenne's in danger," Hunter said, suddenly understanding. "The Rippling is trying to consume her."

"Yes. She carries divine light, the same light you have. The light that makes you fixed points. The Rippling seeks to devour that light. To corrupt it. Turn it into more darkness." Hugo's purple eyes blazed. "If she's consumed, the timelines collapse forever. No more second chances. No more reincarnation. Just void."

Hunter felt his body solidifying. Becoming real again. The chevrons across his skin pulsed brighter, responding to his determination. "What do I have to do?"

"You already know." Hugo's voice was gentle. "You must become what you were always meant to be. Not Ouroboros. Not human. Something new. A bridge between mortality and eternity. You must sacrifice your physical form to power the tablet. Let it consume you. Transform you into pure energy."

"And that will free Evelyne? Save Solenne?"

"Yes. Your dissolution will shatter the Jar. Your energy will push back the Rippling. Your sacrifice will give them the power to survive. To carry on your legacy. To fight The Sovereign when they return."

Hunter looked at the void around him. Saw fragments of his life scattered across infinite possibilities. Saw Tara laughing at their kitchen table. Saw Ember's first steps. Saw Evelyne's face when she realized who he was. Saw Solenne crying in the parking garage, alone, terrified, still fighting because that's what Persefonis did, they fought.

All of it real. All of it happening simultaneously in the quantum space where fixed points existed.

truly was, an ancient being that had guided countless souls through impossible transformations, that had watched universes be born and die, that had chosen to wear the form of a small man with clothespins because sometimes the most powerful things came in humble packages.

"You have chosen well, Hunter Persefoni. Your daughter will know. Your wife will know. And they will carry on your light."

The void erupted with brilliance.

The tablet's power surged through Hunter. Through every scattered piece of him that existed across infinite timelines—pulling him apart atom by atom, memory by memory, heartbeat by heartbeat.

He felt his consciousness expanding.

Fragmenting.

Scattering like light through infinite prisms.

In one timeline, he was holding Ember as a baby, feeling her tiny heart beat against his chest.

In another, he was kissing Tara on their wedding day, tasting strawberries and champagne and forever.

In a third, he was meeting Evelyne for the first time, seeing her green eyes and knowing, just knowing she was important.

In a fourth, he was teaching Solenne to ride a bike in Central Park, her laugh echoing across the Great Lawn.

All of it happening simultaneously.

All of it him.

All of it real.

And then transformation.

His physical body dissolved into pure light. Golden energy that exploded outward in every direction, crossing dimensions, breaking through barriers, shattering the crystal prison that held the woman he loved.

▬▬

Outside the Ambulance - 11:53 p.m.

Solenne stumbled backward as the Jar in her hands began to glow. Not just glow, burn. Pure golden light poured from the crystal, warm against her palms, pulsing in rhythm with a heartbeat she recognized. Dad.

The Jar trembled. Cracks appeared. Thin lines of blazing gold spread across the surface like lightning frozen in crystal.

"No, no, no." Solenne clutched it tighter, afraid it would shatter and she'd lose her mother again. "Please hold together. Please."

The Jar exploded. Not violently. Beautifully. Like a flower made of light blooming in her hands, petals of crystal and gold unfolding in impossible geometry. The fragments hung suspended. A thousand shards catching the parking garage's fluorescent lights, each one reflecting a different timeline, a different possibility, a different version of the family she'd lost and found and lost again.

Then the fragments dissolved into pure light. And Evelyne stood where the Jar had been.

She gasped like she'd been drowning for weeks, pulling air into lungs that had forgotten how to breathe. Her clothes were tattered, the same business suit she'd worn when she activated the Jar, now torn and stained. Her dark hair was wild, tangled. But her eyes, those brown eyes that were also Tara's eyes, merged across timelines into something both familiar and new. Blazed with power and relief and rage.

"Mom." Solenne's voice broke.

Evelyne's head snapped toward her. For a moment, she didn't seem to recognize her own daughter. Too many timelines bleeding together, too many memories from the Jar where she'd been forced to watch infinite realities unfold without being able to touch them.

Her face showed confusion. Then shock. Then recognition.

Then her face crumpled.

"Solenne." The name came out as a sob. "Oh God, Solenne."

They collided.

Mother and daughter. Both crying. Both laughing. Holding each other as the Rippling's dark tendrils retreated from the golden light, as the ambulance behind them began to dissolve—its purpose served, its existence no longer needed—as reality stabilized around them.

"You're real," Solenne sobbed into her mother's shoulder. "You're really real. I was so scared. I thought—when the Jar started breaking, I thought I'd lose you again."

"Shh. I'm here. I'm here now." Evelyne stroked her daughter's hair, and Solenne realized her mother was shaking. "How long was I in there? It felt like years. Centuries. Watching timelines unfold. Watching you grow up in infinite variations. Watching Hunter transform. I tried so hard to break free, but the crystal—"

"Three weeks," Solenne said. "You've been trapped for three weeks."

"Three weeks." Evelyne laughed, but it came out broken. "It felt like forever."

They held each other for a long moment. Then Evelyne pulled back, looking around the parking garage with sharp, assessing eyes that Solenne remembered from childhood. The look that meant Mom was scanning for threats, calculating possibilities, planning their next move.